LIFERS

Jeff Somers

CREATIVE ARTS BOOK COMPANY
BERKELEY ⊘ CALIFORNIA

For information contact:
Creative Arts Book Company
833 Bancroft Way
Berkeley, California 94710

Library of Congress Cataloging-in-Publication Data

Somers, Jeff, 1971-
    Lifers : a novel / Jeff Somers.
        p. cm.
    ISBN 0-88739-322-5 (pbk. : alk. paper)
    1. Young men--Fiction. 2. Publishers and publishing--Fiction. 3.
Male friendship--Fiction. 4. New York (N.Y.) --Fiction. 5. Generation
X--Fiction. 6. Robbery--Fiction.   I. Title.
    PS3619.064 L5 2001
    813".6--dc21

                                          2001028148

Printed in the United States of America

LIFERS

1. Prologue

CHEAP WOMEN ARE THE HOLY GRAIL of many a young man's life. As I sat in Joe Odd's Roost nursing a beer and working through a pack of unfiltereds, waiting for Trim and Danny to show up and tell me, laughing over beers, that everything had gone as planned, I thought about the irony quotient rising all around me. Recently, I'd spent a great deal of my life wishing for cheap women, and now that I was in this crummy bar with women being the last things on my mind, a cheap one sat next to me and asked me to buy her a whiskey sour at three o'clock in the afternoon. She was a peroxide vision in a short black skirt, red blouse, and day-old make-up. She looked like she'd sobered up three times that day already, and wasn't happy about it.

"Isn't it a little early for hard liquor, Mom?" I asked.

"Look," she said with heavy, heavy effort, as if having to explain herself were some form of disrespect, "we're in a bar; you don't come in here to stay sharp. You want to spare a five spot for me or you like to drink alone?"

I sipped some warm beer. "I ain't here to drink, Mom."

"What for, then?"

"I'm waiting for some friends."

"Well," she said with a chuckle approaching genuine humor, "buy me a drink and tell me why."

I bought her a drink. And told her about my lunch with Trim a few months ago.

Trim and I had lunch every week to talk about our writing careers, or, usually, our lack of careers. Trim was a poet; I wrote a lot of things but mostly short fiction. It didn't matter; we got together to bitch about not selling a goddamn thing and to tell each other we were geniuses, which neither of us believed, quite sensibly.

We had no money between us that week so we were eating burgers, sitting outside in the sun smoking cigarettes, sucking on milk shakes, feeling decadent. We were both wearing our sunglasses, because, damn it, we were *artists*. Artists with square jobs, sure, but artists anyway.

Trim has dyed blonde hair and is a tall, gaunt asshole with nothing nice to say about anyone, including himself. He writes incomprehensible poetry that always leaves me feeling creepy and ill-used, which is why I think it's good. His one rule of poetry is that he never uses the word 'love' in his poems. I think it's a good rule. When the conversation veers away from our mutually angst-ridden lives, all Trim does is make fun of people, which is another reason we've been friends since school.

"Harry, that prick," he was saying around his cheeseburger. Trim worked as a video store clerk, making just enough to pay rent and buy beer. Harry was the owner, and as far as I knew he'd been a prick his whole life. "Fucker thinks I don't have anything better to do but alphabetize slasher movies."

I chewed a french fry contemplatively. "You *don't* have anything better to do, really."

He ignored me. "The little shit has me and Jamie working twelve hours each, and he just sits at home and jerks
off. I have proof."

On Saturdays, Trim took off work early and read poems
at the bar around the corner from my apartment. I hated
most of his other friends: a bunch of dyed-hair dressed-in-
black-and-waiting-to-die poets, each of them digging
through musty books looking for the most obscure refer-
ence, the most idiotically scholarly way to say that you'd
rather you'd died before you were born. I stopped by to
hear Trim read and we would hang around afterward to
drink and make fun of the rest of them, which, oddly, made
us favorites there.

"We shouldn't have to work, man." he groused. "If I
could just sit at home and write, I'd—"

"Sit at home and jerk off. I have proof."

He tossed a fry at me. "Don't you ever want to quit that
fucking job of yours?"

"Hell, I get more writing done at work than not. I spend
too many nights drinking with you."

"Hmmph."

I worked as a copy editor at a small publishing house.
Very small, like my salary, which got me a slightly bigger
apartment than Trim and Danny's and, strangely enough,
more bills.

Trim looked down at his burger for a few minutes. "Phil,
our lives are shit, aren't they?"

"Speak for yourself."

"Blow me. You shlep to a job you hate and spend a lot
of time doing things you don't want to do. You waste more
time when you get home drinking beer with me, you spend

about six minutes a fucking day doing what you supposedly love. Your life sucks, and the sad part is that you don't even know it."

The saddest part really was, I did know it. I'd known it for months. We all knew it. We were dying inside, the lot of us, rotting away by steady increments of paychecks, health insurance, rent, and cigarettes.

Lunch was over, but we were still sitting there. Trim was looking at me with his blank sunglasses eyes.

"Okay," I said. "Thanks for tearing me down."

He leaned forward and stole my cigarette, which was a favorite trick of his. "You know what we ought to do?"

I leaned forward and stole it back. "What?"

He nodded happily, as if his head had come loose. "We ought to turn to a life of crime."

"Good thing I brought my gun," I said. "We can start here."

The bastard stole my cigarette again. "I'm serious."

And so we decided to become criminals.

Her name was Norma and I'd bought her two drinks. She was staring at me in a way that hinted her headache wasn't quite gone yet.

"Just like that?" she asked.

I had given up and ordered another beer. "Well, no. It's not like we just ripped off the burger joint and started murdering people. But that was when the idea began. If Trim and I weren't such old friends, that might have been where it ended."

Trim's real name was Damien Harris, but when I'd met him in college he told everyone to call him Trim. A few years later I asked him who had started calling him that, and he'd promptly replied, "I did."

We'd both been English majors, but we were different people. Trim liked to stay up all night drinking shots of tequila and discussing the genius of Frank O'Hara; I liked to sleep late and noodle about with experimental fiction, introducing myself as a writer. I liked to take creative writing classes and tell everyone how much they sucked; he just liked to tell everybody how much they sucked.

We were roommates for a while, but we couldn't stand each other so we gave that up and ended up with worse roommates, which made us both realize how silly life is, sometimes. Two months after our decision to split up we met at a party and spent the night in the kitchen smoking cigarettes and not drinking. We decided to move in together again, because even if we irritated each other at least we knew we weren't psychopaths. Trim's new roommate had recently searched through all of Trim's possessions without even bothering to hide the fact, and furthermore had grown violent when accused. Trim and I lived together for three years once we realized we didn't have to like each other, and so naturally we became friends.

There has always been a cracked charm about Trim that made him likable despite his defects. Trim was the inventor and biggest proponent of the Theory of Diminishing Returns. It was the one reason I knew I had to stay in touch with the bastard. It was deceptively simple: *don't do anything until someone notices that you aren't doing it.*

It can be applied to almost every aspect of your life: professional, romantic, artistic, whatever. Trim's idea was that if you start doing something because you think you ought to, it soon becomes policy. Wait until someone tells you what the policy is, and you end up saving yourself a lot of effort. While I have never been able to apply this in my own life, it remains a revolutionary concept, and I have high hopes that someday it will change the world as we know it, leaving sloths such as myself behind.

After school we each lacked the inertia to actually do anything, so we got jobs in the city, found separate apartments, and began drinking. Being twenty-three and employed is a heady thing; it takes about two years for the bills to hit and until then nothing beats waking up in bars and throwing up at friends' houses. Trim and I have hung out so much that we are actually incapable of any strong feeling towards each other, positive or negative. I neither loved nor hated Trim—I merely knew him so well I often completed his sentences. My other friends regarded him as an accident of the Dr. Spock era of child rearing: they detested him for his arrogance, lack of social skills, and eerie tendency to always speak as if he were quoting. My friend Rachel once told me she suspected he wrote down lines of dialogue in advance and used them as needed. The scariest part of that was how possible it sounded. As a result, the only other person on the East Coast who knew Trim well enough to comment on him was his roommate, Dan, our third partner.

"Guy sounds like a prince," Norma slurred. We were getting to be good friends, Norma and I. She was getting into my cigarettes now, and I suspected that I was something of an answered prayer for her.

"Trim's a stand-up guy in his own way," I answered. "Not many people can get past his bullshit, but if you can, he's a good guy, if something of a sociopath."

"A what?" she asked, taking a heavy pull on her fourth whiskey sour. She had scooted her barstool closer, and I was getting nervous that Norma thought I might be picking her up.

"He manipulates people, or tries to. He treats people like pieces on a board," I explained, though I doubt she was really listening.

"Bummer."

I looked at her. She was maybe forty-something, probably twice my age, and she was canny enough to glom a drink when she could. I didn't know anything about her and didn't want to know, and suddenly felt really creepy about the whole afternoon. I glanced at my watch; Dan and Trim were half an hour late, and I was starting to get worried.

"That's why it's amazing that he and Danny get along as well as they do," I said, to fill in the gap. I had a feeling that everyone in the bar, all seven of them, was listening in.

"Yeah?"

I nodded, sipping beer. "In his own dirty way, Dan's a fucking saint."

Daniel Quinn was a rarity: a truly nice guy, albeit going slightly brown around the edges in his mid-twenties. Fill a guy with beer and coat him with rejection often enough, and even the nicest guys will wither into something more resembling a bastard. Dan had enough mothers-milk niceness in him to go another ten years before becoming a real bastard, but he was beginning to show bastard tendencies, and everyone who knew him simultaneously rejoiced and despaired at the thought.

Trim had answered an ad for a roommate, and I'd gone

along on the interview/lunch, so we met Danny Boy at the same moment. Dan chose a local Mexican joint and wore a pair of tan khakis, a white oxford, and boat shoes. He shook our hands warmly, asked us to have a seat, and asked Trim if he'd like to order drinks. Trim looked him over from head to foot, and said "Own stock in J Crew, huh?"

I was ready right there and then to get up and shake Dan's hand, wish him well, and hustle Trim out of there like the good handler I was, but to my amazement Dan laughed and asked Trim if he wrote poetry or sang in a band. "Only pretentious bastards like that dress like you, chum."

And Trim laughed at that, and roommates were born. We were all supposed to get back to work after lunch, but we got drunk anyway, and Dan told us he wanted to become more of a deviant. Trim confessed he'd once voted but wasn't proud, and I admitted I had a thing for parochial schoolgirls. We were most shocked by Trim's political activities. Hell, *I* hadn't even known about that.

I helped Trim move in three days later, which meant I carried one of the two duffel bags Trim kept all his stuff in. Dan had the place (a tiny but well-kept basement place downtown) packed with used furniture, so Trim didn't need anything else. Dan was most excited by the fact that Trim could get free movies from the video store. That was the sort of guy Dan was, before he met us.

"So what, are you robbing banks?" Norma asked with a cackle that would have attracted attention anywhere but Joe Odd's Roost.

I had long ago come to regret starting a conversation with Norma. She was loud and obnoxious, unattractive and pugnacious. Add to that the fact that the bar lacked sufficient patrons to keep our conversation a secret, and I was quickly becoming desperate to get rid of her, which I guess is a low and dirty thing to think, but hell, that was me.

"Do I look like a bank robber?" I asked with a hint of irritation.

She gave me the foot-to-head treatment, real slow. "Well, you don't look like a criminal at all, Honey," she cackled. "So who knows what the truth is."

I had to grant her the point.

"Not bank robbers—something a little less violent, I guess. We are just a bunch of kids, after all."

She snorted. "You're telling *me*."

Danny Boy was as Irish as they came, which meant he could drink with the best of them and that he had challenged Trim to no less than seven fights in their time together, and counting. I think Trim stayed conscious long enough to take two punches, once. Trim, who had been taking school-yard beatings since he'd been old enough to have a fashion sense, took this aspect of his relationship with Dan in stride. He generally extorted large amounts of cash from a guilty Dan the next day.

Three days after Trim and I decided to become criminals, Dan went through one of the most vicious two-punches life can hand a guy. Within two days, he was dumped by his girlfriend and fired from his job, stripped of his spear, which leaves most men with a vacant stare and little else by way of dignity.

We took him out drinking after he got dumped to make him feel better, and after a few stiff ones I let it slip that Trim and I were plotting to break laws. Trim was aghast at my lack of discretion, but Dan was hurt that we hadn't trusted him, which melted Trim's reserve. After all, Dan had been dumped by Meredith Simmons and dumped badly, and he deserved some amount of pity. Not only deserved it, but needed it and was apt to complain if he didn't get it.

Meredith was a striking redhead who wasn't Irish but wished to be. You see a lot of that, actually: Irish is one of the few ethnic groups that nice white girls can aspire to without upsetting their dads, unless Dad is an avowed John Bull. Irish is a popular feel for many white kids who lack ethnic identities but want one; you'll find Polocks drinking pints, Wops wearing claddagh rings. Why, I have no idea. I'm half-Irish myself, and I don't consider it my attractive half.

Meredith was bossy, crass, and tasteless, but beautiful. Dan dated her because he was amazed that a shlep like him could manage to hang on to a beautiful girl like Meredith, but he didn't love her. None of us did. Who could? She began every conversation with "You know what I think," and ended every conversation with "I don't give a shit anyway," and was more concerned with being the It Girl of the moment than with forging any kind of emotional bond with anyone, including Dan and not excluding the rest of us. Still, it's the bossy and crass girls that tie you up in knots most times, so it isn't surprising that when she finally dumped Dan he was ruined for a few days. Deep in our cups, Trim watched in horror as I told Dan that we were tired of selling ourselves piecemeal and wanted to become criminals—at the very least take control of our lives.

Aside from being shocked, he was doubtful.

"You idiots can't even pay your bills on time," he said around a beer. "How can you plan a crime? Shall I buy files to bring you now, or should I wait?"

Trim was indignant. "Listen up, you fucking Mick, just because you can't manage to hold down a job doesn't mean Dub and me are morons, too. We're not talking about ripping off gas stations, you shit."

Dan hadn't heard the last part. He was standing, weaving slightly, and staring at Trim with small eyes I'd seen before. I looked around the bar and started to edge away.

"Who you calling a fucking moron?" Dan demanded.

Trim knew he'd made an error. Trim was no fighter; he preferred to sit in darkened theaters and throw popcorn at kids six or seven rows ahead. "Dan," he said, standing up carefully, "that isn't what I meant, man. I just—"

And Dan hit him, spinning Trim around and sending him to the floor gracelessly. Trim stayed down. Aside from being a fey poet whose dark side, I had learned, is half-bullshit, Trim had a glass jaw. Dan looked around carefully, and sat down with immense drunken care. After a long, breathless pull on his beer, he glanced at me.

"So what's the plan, Scarface?"

I shrugged. "We don't have one. Yet."

He blinked at me, slow and deliberate, once, and then broke into braying laughter. I glanced down at Trim, then joined in.

Trim came up swinging two hours later, but was mollified to learn that Dan was in the bathroom puking his guts out. Dan'd had just enough left in the tank to help carry Trim home, and had promptly turned liquid. I was sitting in the living room smoking and feeling myself sober up when Trim popped up, a nasty bruise along his cheek and a wild look in his eye.

"Filthy bastard," he muttered after a quick search revealed no Dan. "I guess he fled."

I exhaled smoke. "In the john, reliving the evening. Loudly."

Trim cradled his head delicately. "You don't suppose he's going to turn us in, do you?"

I grinned. "We haven't done anything. We don't even have a plan yet, for Christ's sake."

Trim, in his way, was not convinced that this was a problem. According to the Theory of Diminishing Returns, attitude was half the battle. According to the Phil Dublen Theory of Hard Knocks, attitude like that got your balls cut off.

Dan had passed out, and in the moment of crystal silence I stood up. "Gotta go, gotta work tomorrow."

Trim just stared at the floor. "You fucking suburbanite."

Joe Odd's Roost was a bar with a split personality. On the weekends it was close enough to everything to be a relatively hip bar where a lot of young, promising kids came to ruin their potential. On the weekdays, it was a dreary place filled with a smattering of those who have no potential, or who have squandered all they once had. On Saturday nights its red bricks and old jukebox were charming; on Saturday nights after a few pitchers of beer they were downright homey. On Thursday afternoon with Norma starting to act like my date it was depressing, because I was hunched over the bar just like all the other losers, and if I wasn't as drunk as they were at three in the afternoon, I still looked just like them.

"You live around here, Phiby?"

I considered my possibilities. Trim and Dan were late, so

I had no idea how long I was going to be sitting there, breathing Norma's air and melting into my barstool. There are two terrible things about sitting in a cheap bar in the middle of the day: sitting alone with only your thoughts for company, and sitting with someone else as pathetic as you are. You just couldn't win.

I looked at Norma askance. "You picking me up, Norma?"

A snake-like foot edged along my calf. I fell off of my stool, and Norma burst into cackling laughter. It continued, impressively, as I climbed back up. The laugh degenerated into a wet cough, and I sucked beer in self-defense.

"Don't worry, pretty boy. I won't seduce you," she cackled.

I sat and stared while she caught her breath, what she had left after all these years. For a moment I gloried in silence.

"Why're you doing this, baby?" she suddenly wanted to know.

I considered really telling her, about Chick and Mom and Trim and Christine and my own stupid little dissatisfactions, but instead I summoned some grim irony. "Isn't crime the great American Dream?" I answered, wittily enough, I thought. Wit, however, was lost on Norma and her silent partners.

"I thought you kids were writers," she slurred.

I stared at my beer for a moment, feeling quiet and suddenly depressed. "Well, Norma, maybe I forgot to mention something. There was one more reason why the idea of becoming crooks appealed to us."

"Yeah?" she asked blurrily. "What?"

I sighed. "We aren't very good writers."

There was a party shortly after that, if I recall correctly; but there were always parties somewhere, and we usually got invited to them, despite Trim's tendency to make dark jokes about people's physical deficiencies, my tendency to hit on all the chicks (unsuccessfully, of course, but with a great deal of cheer), and Dan's tendency to kill the kegs. Actually, considering the entertainment value of our activities, maybe we were invited because of them.

This party was thrown by Chick Parker, who was a waitress at Rue's Morgue, one of the bars that Trim accosted with his poetry sometimes. Chick had no ambitions beyond living in our neighborhood, waitressing, and partying for the rest of her youth, and then getting married at the last minute of her thirties and giving it all up. She was cute, and a happy drunk, and she knew everyone, and when she got bored she threw big parties at her loft and invited everyone she knew, which was everyone.

I lusted after Chick. She was short and brunette and slim and she had something smart to say to everyone and everything. I couldn't resist. She could tell you to fuck off and make you like it (or at least, make *me* like it) and very often did. She led me around by my penis all night, patted me on the cheek at the end, and up until we'd decided to become criminals she'd never once hinted that I was anything but possibly the 300th most witty guy she'd ever met.

Dan, Trim, and I (with a drunk fellow snoozing peacefully on the table) had taken over the kitchen, drinking Chick's whiskey in careful jelly glasses and planning our criminal careers. We weren't very popular that night, partly because someone in the room smelled pretty badly of vomit (my second guess was the unconscious fellow) and partly because Trim screamed "Get out you friggin' social vampires!" at everyone who entered, including (sadly) Chick herself, whose eye I had once again failed to catch.

"Let's face it," Dan said with the breathlessness of the very drunk. "We're not really criminals."

"Hell—" Trim started.

"Wait a second," Dan broke in, "and listen to me. I think we have to be realistic about this. I am not carrying a fucking gun."

That stopped Trim with his mouth open. "Okay," he said at last, quietly. "Okay."

We decided to toast this wise decision.

"Whatever we pull, it's got to be big. I'm not risking all this for small change," I said earnestly. This seemed only prudent to me, but Trim started laughing. Bad music floated around us and the hum of conversation insulated us.

"Oh, man," Trim giggled, throwing his arms out and leaning his chair back, "he gestures to 'all this' as if it were a fucking kingdom or something!" He dissolved into laughter. Dan joined him, cackling cheerfully.

"Let's face it, chum," Trim said after a few moments, wiping his eyes. "You ain't risking a goddamn thing."

"No, not yet, anyway," I replied blandly. "We don't even have a goddamn plan."

But we would, very soon.

Dan had worked in the accounting department of a big corporation because he had never had an ambition for anything in particular, and his low-key nihilism had led him straight into cubicle hell. It was the sort of place where they let you wear jeans one day a week and that was supposed to be the cheese in the trap.

Every week, Dan got a memo explaining some detail

of the rules. They always had to keep explaining the details, because people kept finding ways to get around them, loopholes. I imagined, hearing Dan talk, that his company's dress code-slash-behavior guidelines now filled several buildings rented just for that purpose, probably in Jersey. In giddier moments, Dan drew amusing doodles depicting his bosses as Nazis.

We only worked about eight blocks apart, really, in midtown, so after I'd gotten to know him a little the inevitable polite lunch was suggested. The day we had planned it, Dan was really busy but didn't want to cancel on me (me being such scintillating company, you see) and we ended up eating take-out in his company's lunchroom, which was more depressing than it sounds, believe it or not. It was big and roomy and terminally empty and no matter how many people sat in it like little poison islands of silence it didn't fill up. You could have people sitting in the sink it was so fucking crowded and it would still feel empty. It was white and chill and sterile, and Dan and I hardly talked the whole lunch because we didn't feel like we could. I shoveled shredded beef in garlic sauce into my gut, thanked him listlessly, and ran for my life.

Dan hated his job more than I hated mine, more than Trim hated his, because Dan had nothing else. I could feel it as we ate our grim lunch that day: Dan hated it because that was him, that was what defined him. Dan had been potty-trained to always have a good job and to always be working hard at it. He was eating shit every day of his life and he was starting to get a taste for it. And then he got fired, and it was like the Bastards had even taken that away from him. No wonder he became the leader of our little gang.

◎

They were an hour late, and I was losing my small store of small talk. Norma had glommed six stiff drinks off me and was losing interest in me anyway since I'd made no move to buy her a seventh. The place was starting to fill up with the slightly less desperate after-work cocktail crowd, the sort of people who like to start off their grim little evenings with a few drinks. A suit and tie popped in, and I knew we were about an hour away from busy.

I had half a cigarette left, burning effortlessly in my hand, delicate smoke curling around my fingers and rising to the ceiling to mix with smoke stains from a million wasted afternoons, a million endless nights. In that half cigarette, I thought:

we got caught we're all going to jail and my only option right now is where do they catch me, in front of my family, my friends, my coworkers or in the privacy of my home with some small amount of dignity or maybe in action, making the proverbial break for it, though lord knows I haven't got the slightest idea where people make a break for

I can't go back to that job, I can't go back to breathless dashes for nine o'clock and bitter coffee and stupid gossip and hungover status reports and ID cards and dress codes and endless streams of paper paper paper I used to love paper so much it used to be my foil, my canvas, and now it's just what I do I couldn't go back there and suck it up, I was bloated on suck already I just couldn't do it

where the fuck are they

too many people in this fucking bar I'd been here sixty or seventy billion Friday nights I once even got lucky in here with that girl Sharon or Sherry or something who came in and came on to me when her boyfriend pissed her off and I bought her kamikazes and we started making out and when her boyfriend called her a cunt she decided to fuck me in revenge and I remember not liking the feeling not that it stopped me

I can't go to jail

oh shit what if someone I know shows up what the hell were we thinking meeting in a place we've been before and might be known at Jesus Christ we're morons no wonder it all fucking fell apart

Christ I think they're watering down the beer in here anyway

I never noticed all the pictures on the walls here I wonder if those are real people or not

and then the cigarette was done, down to the filter, and I exhaled smoke, tossed a fiver onto the bar, and stood up to leave. We hadn't made a plan "B," so I made one up on the spot: get the hell out of there and practice amnesia.

I walked outside, and the sudden sunlight hit me hard and I closed my eyes. I stood there blinking for a moment, then started to run.

2. The Plan

Trim was trying to catch a cigarette in his mouth, and failing every time. I was watching him in mixed fascination and horror, thinking of those monkeys they lock in cages to OD themselves on drugs by pushing a button. Dan was cooking us all Spaghetti-Os in their little kitchen, and my stomach turned at the thought. I was hungover from my night before, and dimly I knew that if I were to explore that part of myself, I'd find that when I am invited over for dinner I do not expect to get Spaghetti-Os.

We were sitting silently at the card table they had in the living room, not saying anything because Trim and I had run out of conversation around Tuesday of the week before. The only thing worth talking about we didn't want to open up.

Their apartment was dark and musty, with the same carpeting and decorations that generations of idiotic young men and women had lived with. It was the sort of cheap, fleabag apartment that got passed on from broke young kids to broke younger kids every couple of years, and no one had ever bothered to clean the fucking place before they moved their shit in and grew too tired. Trim often boasted that he'd taught the roaches to be his servants and that they worshiped him as an otherworldly ruler. In a bar, that was passably amusing. In Trim's actual apartment, it wasn't.

There was a crash and a volley of cursing from the kitchen. I looked at Trim, Trim tried again to catch a cigarette on its way down to the floor, and that was the sum of our conversation.

Dan brought out dinner and a few beers, sat down with us, and didn't say anything either. I took a spoonful of the muck and examined it with a trained eye, returning it to the bowl without comment. I lit a cigarette, opened my beer, and watched Dan and Trim not eat either for a few seconds.

"Well," I said without preamble, not having enough words in me to string one together, "what's up?"

Dan put down the spoon he hadn't been using and glanced around the room. Finally he looked back at me. "I have an idea."

Trim snickered. "Glory be. I've been waiting for this day for years."

Dan shot him a look, but Trim just stared at him. You could hit Trim pretty hard and he wouldn't be impressed. He wasn't much of a fighter, but he also wasn't intimidated by a beating, which I found an admirable trait. Besides, Dan still felt guilty over his latest drunken exploit with Trim, and grimaced in shame after a moment under Trim's crazy eyes.

"It's about . . . our plan."

I was honestly perplexed for a moment. It had been a week since Chick's party, and I had started to think of our flirtation with crime as an intellectual vanity, a fun thing to think about but something none of us had taken seriously, like a million other things Trim and I had discussed, including: moving to Mexico, growing pot in our dorm room to sell, and becoming porno actors. They were the sort of virtual reality schemes that seemed totally possible and within our meager powers . . . until two weeks went by and we had forgotten all about it.

Dan, however, seemed to have reached a point where it wasn't just a mental exercise anymore. Maybe it was collecting unemployment. Maybe it was sleeping alone and whacking off in the bathroom again after all those years of dating Meredith. He reached over and stole my cigarette, leaning back like he'd been memorizing Bogart movies all day.

"You mean the crime of the century?" I asked, surprised.

He nodded, and then blinked. "You guys were serious, right?"

I glanced at Trim and he glanced at me. We hung in stasis for a moment, and then a slow-witted, demented little grin eased itself across his crinkly face and I knew that this was one of those golden moments Trim had spent his life waiting for. He looked over at Dan and leaned across to steal my cigarette from him. I don't think either one of the bastards had bought a pack in all the years I'd known them.

"Thank God," Trim said happily. "I've corrupted you at last."

I gave up and gave in, lighting a new cigarette. "What was your idea?" I asked.

Dan smiled shyly. "Think about your job . . . "

My job: paper, paper everywhere, and I saw every single goddamned sheet, let me tell you. I had zero ambition, and it showed in my late arrivals, unshaven countenance, and the fact that when I had my last review and had not been offered a raise I merely shrugged and asked if I was free to go. Being successful at your job was the cheapest form of fulfillment there was. Dedicating your life to your employment was for those who liked to court life but wilted at the sight of her parted, smooth thighs; the poseurs who had so little originality in them that they accepted someone else's goals as their own and smiled happily around the gruel.

It was a large publishing house, over five hundred employees in the New York office, and I was one of them, a junior member of the comma counters and style gurus, a nameplate and a cubicle. I wore a tie to work and was well-liked, I hated my job with every scrap of dignity I had left, and by the end of the day I had computer-squint and writer's cramp. But that wasn't what interested Dan.

"Remember last Christmas?" he prompted.

I closed my eyes. "I got two videotapes I still haven't watched, a couple of books I've read and forgotten, three shirts from aunts—"

"No, at your *job*." he interrupted me.

Christmas at my job: we were ordered to attend our party, which was a snazzy affair held in a nice hotel. Free drinks, bad food, limp music, but we had no choice, which was what irked me, which was what drove me to drink too many drinks and stand up on a chair and begin what would have been a scathing retirement speech had I not fallen off and hit the floor hard.

Traditionally, we got a Christmas bonus. But where other companies usually gave a percentage of your salary in a bogus but meaningful gesture of appreciation, our tradition remained at its original level: a crisp fifty-dollar bill. Every employee, from the vice presidents on down, received fifty dollars in cash, as they had for fifty-three years, the legacy of our founder and patron saint. All it meant to us employees was that when we hit a bar after the lame party none of us had anything smaller than a fifty to break.

It was a grim, small life. I often tried to enlarge it; at the last Christmas debacle, I'd invited Trim and Dan out to the bar afterward, luring them with a promise of fifty dollars of free drinks. I'd gotten famously bombed (I still felt lingering brain damage from the subsequent hangover if I sat up too quickly) and while walking home the need to throw up became a religious quest. Dan and Trim had happily taken me to my office to do so. We'd gotten in without a problem, and there was no one around at all. The place had been deserted, down to the security guard who was half in a bag in the little office they were supposed to stay out of.

I can remember waving to the happy old bastard when we left, feeling gray but cheerful.

I looked at Dan steadily and finished my beer, getting up automatically to get another. After all, all I had to worry about the next day was work. "Okay, your point?"

Dan leaned back. None of us had even touched his carefully prepared Spaghetti-Os. "My Uncle Tom is out of stir again."

I glanced at Trim, but Trim was still grinning, sitting there smoking another of my cigarettes, looking wise. Or possibly sleeping with his eyes open, a skill he often boasted of. I popped open my beer and gave Dan another few seconds.

"So? Your Uncle Tom's always been a crook, Dan."

◎

All white Catholic families have at least one jailbird. I'm not sure why this is, but it's absolutely true. The Kennedys, for Christ's sake, have crooks in their brood—the crooks are just a little bit more high class, more David Niven in *The Pink Panther* than Dan's Uncle Tom.

My cousin Frankie stole cars, and was damned good at it, too. At every interminable family get-together Frankie was trying to give me a car, usually a Trans Am or some other testosterone nightmare. Once he'd tried to give me an Iroc with the words *babe-o-rama* detailed on the rear window; he really seemed to think the detailing was a selling point. Frankie meant well; despite his criminal tendencies and eighth-grade education, not to mention a bad habit of getting knifed in bars and causing Aunt Caroline several heart attacks, he only wanted to take care of his family. Frankie viewed me as that sad breed of man who couldn't steal his own cars, and he felt sorry for me.

The funny thing was, with these black sheep, we didn't really treat them like shameful elements. They were "characters."

I had met Dan's Uncle Tom once: he'd been slumming around Dan's Mom's house one Sunday when we'd driven up there. I don't recall why we'd gone, only that the car (the ancient and despised Chevette, which had preceded Dan's ancient and despised Malibu) had wheezed into his Mom's driveway and had promptly emitted a thick cloud of black smoke and died, sadly. Tom was fortyish, beer-gutted, and had a way of looking at you with a crazy half-mast stare that made you wonder how many times he'd been raped in prison.

Sitting outside Mom's house that night, waiting with Trim and Dan for the useless and expectedly rude triple-A guy, I asked Dan what his uncle had done to get put in jail for three years, six months, and some amount of days. Dan had looked at me seriously and said, "Office supplies."

"Exactly!" Dan said, pounding the table. He should have been smiling in triumph, but he wasn't. I looked at Trim, but Trim was still smiling like something was directly massaging his brain.

"Uncle Tom fences stolen stuff. My Mom once told me all about it. I think she secretly admires her crook brother. He's the baby of the family, so . . .

"Anyway," Dan continued, "Tom waits for people to bring him stolen goods and he buys them." He sat back. "That simple."

"That simple?" I asked, staring around the room in comic shock. "What's the rest?"

Trim put his cigarette into his mouth, leaned across the table, and hit me lightly on the side of my head. "You idiot: we rob your job. After the Christmas party."

"Exactly!" Dan repeated, pounding the table grimly.

We would need: someone else's ID card to open all the doors. My increasingly paranoid and penny-pinching company had outfitted the whole place with endless security, tedious and insulting. Every time you opened a door in the place a computer logged you: they knew when you showed up and when you left. Scary. It wouldn't do to be listed as present in the building the same moment in time that the place got robbed, so it was up to me to steal someone's ID card on the day of The Caper. Any earlier and we'd risk the victim noticing and having the card removed from the system.

We would need: an alibi. This, we thought, might be difficult, but Trim made a little speech about how people get fuzzy when they drank a lot, so . . .

We would need: a lot of cash, to buy drinks. We planned on taking everyone out after my office party and getting every last Christian and Pagan soul smashed. This would, we hoped, make it impossible for anyone to forget that we'd been there, and impossible to remember when we'd left.

We would need: a van or truck. Small enough not to be noticed, but big enough to carry dozens of computers, typewriters, fax machines, et cetera. Something we could fill up, transport with safety, and get rid of quickly.

We would need: someplace to meet Tom at, to unload the stuff, and get our quick payoff. That, as far as I was concerned, was up to Tom. I felt winded just thinking about it all, so Tom could do a little thinking for us. He had more experience, anyway.

I toasted them with beers, and they clinked glasses, Trim with an obscene wink and Dan with the same grim set-in-stone expression he'd always had. We sat for a moment, watching each other, and it seemed to me that for the first time I really saw these guys I'd only known, really, for about five or six years. Well, Trim, at least; Dan I'd known for maybe two. Dan was bland on first impression, but looking at him there I saw a lot more: the small scar under his eye and the crooked nose that hinted at a few childhood fights, the bright green of his eyes that gave him a powerful stare whether he realized it or not, the fact that I'd never seen him with his mouth hanging open, not once, oddly enough.

Trim, for all his dyed-blonde hair and smart-assed smile,

had warm brown eyes and a way of crinkling them at you that made you think he was a good guy even when he was treating you like shit. Trim pissed me off more often than not, but I loved the bastard. He was like a craggly, beaten old dog: he growled at you, but on cold winter nights he curled up around your feet and fell asleep, and you'd sit there and let your butt fall asleep rather than disturb him.

I started to laugh. That was Trim: a big dog.

3. Conversation

WE DID NOT EXACTLY LEAP INTO ACTION.
We had three months to plan and bicker, mostly bicker.

Two weeks later we met for a drink after work (Dan after a day spent working temp jobs just to keep his hand in on the rent until our score came through) and I wondered how much we stood to make off this thing.

"Not enough to retire on," Dan asserted, "but enough to start something with, maybe. Ten grand each, maybe. Maybe more. We'll have to talk to Uncle Tom and get estimates, I guess."

We were doing this by the seat of our pants. "What'll you do with that cash?"

Trim snickered. "Wine, women, and song, of course."

Dan was aghast. "You'll waste it?"

Trim shrugged. "Waste it? Why not? I'm a criminal now; there'll be other scores. Why should I treat this money differently than the money I've been wasting my whole life?"

"I'm going to invest it," I said solemnly. "Get a nest egg going."

Trim stared at me. "I don't believe it. You're going to keep *working*?"

"Sure," I replied. "What else can I do? Ten grand—if we get that much—isn't exactly the lottery."

"Oh, *man*." Trim spat. "Weren't you listening when I had this idea? This isn't about money, for Christ's sake. This is about reclaiming your life, about getting back some time for yourself. If you just keep working then all this is just another job."

"This *is* about money," Dan said, quietly.

"Damned right it is," I agreed quickly. "All that shit you talk about, Damien, all that happy hippie bullshit about freedom and reclaiming your life, it comes down to how much money do you have? If any of us were truly looking to be fucking "free," we'd be drifting, living off the fatta the land."

Trim studied me. "It's not hippie horseshit. It's more new age."

We laughed, breaking the tension between friends who for a few seconds weren't sure they really knew each other. Arguing over beers is never wise; tempers flare and minor philosophical differences become huge gulfs, and fists fly. Sad.

"Seriously, though," Trim went on, his impish face looking anything but serious, "this isn't about money for me. Money comes and goes. This is a whole new way of looking at things, for me. Instead of playing by these fucking rules, I'm taking a chance and doing it my way."

I looked at Dan, and Dan shrugged at me. "I'm looking to make a little money," I said, and Dan chuckled again.

"What about you, Dan?" Trim suddenly wanted to know.

"Me?" Dan said, looking down at the floor. "I don't think this is about money for me, though I don't mind making a mint off it." He shook his head. "I don't know, I

think I just don't have any other choice. It's either this or
go crazy, you know?"

There was a moment of quiet, then, when I just drank
the rest of my beer fast and pretended not to notice. When
I looked back at them, they were each doing the same
thing. Suddenly, Trim turned back to me with a big smile.
"Hey, Chick Parker just walked in."

I smiled back. "Yeah?"

"Yeah. Let's call her over and see if we can't get her to
sleep with you."

I hate to admit it, but I blushed a little and looked away.
"And how, uh, how do you propose to do that? Exactly?"

Trim winked. "The ancient male magic, mi amigo, the
old and hallowed ceremony that we men have been per-
forming for centuries, worn smooth with use and faded
with age, but still the most powerful ritual we men possess."

"Just fill me in, Einstein."

"We're going to get her drunk," he replied jovially.

This was not so easy with Chick; Chick was a drinker
by profession and so I had little faith in Trim's plan. I was
happy, though, when Trim convinced her to sit with us for
a while, her proud breasts mesmerizing in their own way.
Besides, she was certainly better conversation than Trim
and Dan, who were turning out to be One Trick Ponies in
that regard.

"Hey, Dub, what's up?" she asked brightly, smiling at
Trim as he set a margarita in front of her.

"Nothing," I replied, which was the standard reply. Your
leg could be on fire and you were supposed to start the conversation off with 'nothing.' "Just plotting."

"With these two? Dub, you've got to find a better class of

friends," she said with that delightful crinkle around her eyes. "What are you plotting?"

Trim jumped in. "Chick, maybe you can help us with a philosophical debate?"

She gave him her best wise-woman look. "Certainly." Chick had been involved with sexless flirting at the ground floor of the movement; she'd invented several of the techniques herself and had whole chapters devoted to her in the handbooks. I watched her sip her drink in open admiration, knowing that this was a girl who could teach me things.

"If you were to find a way to cheat the world out of some money," Trim asked with what he thought was a rakish slant, "would you still consider yourself a part of the straight world and keep playing by the rules, or would you cut loose and embrace the chaos?"

This impressed Chick. "Wow. This isn't the usual bar talk, is it?" She leaned back and put her hands behind her head. I bit my lip and kept my eyes on her face. A few seconds later she scanned us, to see which of us might be staring at her chest. I wasn't sure which condition was the passing grade.

"I think I need more details," she said and smiled.

And so Chick Parker became an unknowing confidant. Under the guise of the empty and slightly pathetic alcohol-induced argument, we told her everything. By the end of it, we were all drunk, and glasses and bottles filled our little table. Dan refused to let the poor waitress clear them away.

Chick began to play with my hair, which scared the hell out of me.

"I don't think there's any right or wrong way to follow something like that up," she said, curling a finger around my ear. "I mean, once you do something like that—cross that line—I don't think anything you choose to do afterward can be construed as selling out."

"Thank you," I said solemnly, squeezing her shoulder. She put her hand over mine and held it there.

Trim was slumped over the table with a cigarette burning down to the filter in one hand. "Okay, okay," he said with a cavernous yawn. "You win. Let's go home."

I looked at Chick and felt my heart stand still as she nodded. "Yeah, it's late, and I'm bombed, and I gotta work the lunch shift tomorrow." She stood up, letting my hand slide from hers without comment. I sat, staring into my beer, and looked up at her, just in time to see her swooping in for a chaste peck on the cheek.

"Night, baby," she said sweetly, and then with a cocky swing of her purse she was on her way out. I had a bellyful of beer and an improbable hard-on, considering the hour and the condition I was in, and she was going home to crawl between pink sheets with her bare legs rubbing together cozily, to dream of men most probably not me.

"Sorry, chap," Trim said in a slur as he balanced on the curb. "Usually works. She must not like you that way."

I sighed out smoke. "I don't think she knows I have a penis."

Dan barked laughter on my right, and I scowled at him. It was chilly, and I was only wearing a sports jacket. I tightened up against the wind and ignored Dan, who as usual was a boring drunk.

Trim was revived by the cool air; his hair was sticking up in fine, mussed form, his pale face was split in an honest grin of delight, as if being young, drunk, and alive were the three best things to be in this world. I envied him.

He put an arm around me and continued balancing on the curb as we walked. "Listen, Dub, you've got a serious Best-Friend Syndrome going on, and you've got to stop it, and soon. Or else you'll be on intimate terms with your hand for the rest of your life." He grinned wider. "Or a homosexual."

Dan snorted, and I didn't like the sound of it.

"I know," I said to Trim, "I know. They all think I'm their brother, but—"

"All you want to do is shag 'em!" Trim exulted.

"No," I said, calmly. I thought better of it. "Well, yeah."

He cackled, losing his balance and letting go of me. He stumbled about for a theatrical couple of moments, gasping for air and slapping his knee. "Oh, that's classic," he sputtered, coming back to me, "classic! But listen: you have to stop trying to be such a nice guy. A girl likes a guy who just goes for it."

Sound advice, I figured, but then again, who knew; I was no Alpha male, that was for sure. I stuffed my hands into my pockets and studied my Chucks. "That isn't me, man."

Trim threw a more comradely arm around me. "You're telling *me*," he said warmly.

Dan snorted happily again. "Fag."

A week later, the conversation was still not about our supposed crime. It was as if we'd crossed a line when we'd come up with a concrete idea, and now we were unsure of what to do. I imagined us standing around, smoking cigarettes, toeing the line dubiously.

Trim and I were in Jersey, having lunch at my Mom's house. Mom was a cheerful old woman, a gal who had become old without complaint and who was, I thought, enjoying being old. She was a classic old widow in the sense that she let her son have a private conversation in her ugly kitchen without nosing in. In short, she made us ham sandwiches and went out into the garden.

Trim was stuffing his face, drinking with gusto the weak domestic beer Mom liked, licking mayonnaise off his fingers loudly. Trim enjoyed the pleasures of the flesh more than most people allowed themselves to, and he was one of those bastards who could eat anything and not gain weight, smoke Reds and not get cancer, screw everyone who let down their guard and never get warts on his dick. You either loved Trim despite this or hated him for it. Where I stood on the whole issue depended greatly on whether he was reading one of his poems when you asked me about it.

My Mom had an unwarranted affection for Trim. I think because I'd left most of my childhood friends behind, she saw Trim as that old male buddy I hadn't had for a long while. She even invited him over for holidays, and often bought him gifts.

I think Mom liked Trim better, as a matter of fact.

At any rate, we had chosen Mom's house to have a Caper meeting (*Caper* being Trim's word) but Dan had gotten a call from Meredith, which had given him hope of getting her back, and he'd been off like a shot. I'd tried to get out of the lunch, but Mom was sweetly insistent that she never got to see her boy and his clever friend much anymore, and thus ham sandwiches and weak beer, and Mom popping in from the garden like a phantom.

"How old is your Mom?" Trim asked, leaning back and studying a pickle intently.

I shook my head, chewing carefully. "Too old for you, pervert."

Trim smiled good naturedly, which he did when insulted if he thought the insult particularly inventive. "Aha! An Oedipal Complex, you chivalrous bastard. But no, I'm just curious."

I shrugged. "Sixty-five."

"She just retired last year, huh?"

"Yeah. She's pretty well set."

He nodded. "Did she like her job?"

I stared. "Are you kidding? My god, she hated it. I think she contemplated murdering her boss a few times, judging from her uncharacteristic use of cuss words."

"How long was she there?" he asked, opening a third beer and looking like he would ask for the *TV Guide* any second.

"Thirteen years. She took it to get me through college." I looked down at my plate, with a half-sandwich. I didn't like to think about how hard Mom had worked for me; it made me feel like a heel.

"Hated it for thirteen years, huh?"

Trim was looking at me. I wondered what he'd been like in high school; a geek, sure, but a geek with attitude, probably the sort of geek who was almost as popular as the idiot savants that make up most high school elites. We would never have been friends.

I got up and inspected Mom's liquor cabinet, which was just one of the cabinets above the sink. I found a bottle of

Jim Beam and pulled it out, one guilty eye on Mom, bent over some weeds in the yard. I began to quickly mix a drink.

"What about your Mom?" I asked.

"Dead," he replied instantly.

"Oh yeah. Your Dad?"

"Dead."

"Oh yeah. Did they hate their jobs?"

He snorted. "Hell, yes. That's why they're dead."

I turned, and Trim was looking at me. I guess we were talking about the Caper after all.

Later that night, after the long drive from Mom's house, I called Chick Parker for some conversation and humiliation, not necessarily in that order. I had drunk too much at Mom's to drive, but had driven anyway, and I was lazy and thick-tongued and foolish.

"Hello?"

"Hey."

"Dub? What's up?"

I was in luck; she was drunk too.

"Nothing much. How about you?"

"Nooothing," she cooed. "I'm in bed."

My heart lurched. "This early?"

"I had a date."

Something hinted at possibilities. "And you're home this early?"

She snorted. "It was a bad date."

"I'm sorry."

"It's okay. He was self-involved and inconsiderate, I drank too much wine, and he tried to cop a feel, so I ended the date. Guys are such jerks, you know?"

I said that I did.

"All I wanted was to sit and talk, hear all his dumb stories, tell my own dumb stories, you know? I think that's why we date, really: you have to find new people to tell all your dumb stories to. All my friends yawn and tell me to be quiet when I start repeating my stories, but after a while you've told them all, you know?"

I said I did.

"But the jerk had to ruin it. People suck, sometimes, Dub."

I sighed weightily. "They sure do, Chick."

She smiled. I don't know how I knew, but she did. "Not you, Dub. You're a sweetheart, you know that?"

I stared at the ceiling. I didn't want to hear how sweet I was. "No, I'm not, Chick. But I'll tell you something: I'll listen to your stories, even if I've heard them before."

She sighed. "Thanks. Take care, Dub, I'm fallin' asleep."

"You too," I said. I wanted to say more, but I didn't.

"Take care," she said again, drowsily, and was gone.

I stared at the ceiling some more; it seemed the work I was born to do. I pictured Chick snuggled under her covers and asleep, and before I knew it, I was asleep too.

4. Uncle Tom

MY APARTMENT IS AT THE TOP of a tall, narrow building, and it is a tall, narrow apartment. I'd cleaned and put the place in order, feeling vaguely silly nesting for Dan's creepy uncle. Trim and I sat around and burned cigarettes nervously; Dan appeared to doze with a beer in his hand, not always the same one. When the bell rang Trim and I jumped; Dan merely woke up. I jabbed the buzzer for a healthy period of time, then sat down again, wondering how to appear casual, as if I'd ever known. It took Uncle Tommy a full five minutes to pant his way up the stairs, and by the time he rapped on my door, we were rabid with nerves.

I leapt up and tore the door open.

"No fucking elevator."

Dan's Uncle Tommy was a short, dark man who stared sullenly at the floor at all times, his bulging gut grotesque and impossible to ignore. He had Dan's shifty eyes and nothing else that was Dan's. He was unshaven and tanned and his arms were thick and inflexible. He was about fifty years old and didn't seem to be enjoying himself.

"Come on in," I said gruffly, trying to be tough.

Uncle Tommy glanced around without lifting his head, studying me through his eyebrows for a moment. He moved in slowly, hooked a chair with his foot, and sat down heavily. I let the door shut quietly and turned to him. I was about to offer him a beer, but he already had mine in his hand, and one of my cigarettes.

"Fucking filters," he said disdainfully. He looked over at Dan, or rather right over Dan's shoulder. "Hey, kid."

Dan nodded at him. "Uncle Tommy."

"How's your Dad?"

"Fine."

"I won't fucking bother him with a hello, but tell him I asked about him, huh?"

"Yeah."

I glanced at Trim, but he was smiling his dangerous smile. There was a moment of tense silence, which Tommy broke with a herculean coughing fit. He hacked up something that sounded horrible, tasted it for a moment, and swallowed it down, making me feel a little ill.

"All right," he mumbled. "Dan tells me you got a score on the line."

Trim's grin intensified. "You ever kill anyone?"

Uncle Tommy paused to swivel his eyes over at Trim. He took in Trim's blonde hair, spiky and stiff, his black clothes, and his freaky smile. "You a faggot, kid?"

Trim's eyes crinkled in good humor. "Sometimes. You ever get it done to you in jail?"

Uncle Tommy killed off his beer and crushed the can. "Nope. I paid my way straight. Dan, this guy a joker?" he asked over his shoulder. "I ain't got time for jokers."

Trim opened his mouth, and Uncle Tommy leaned over and slapped him, hard, across the face. When Trim's head whipped back around he found himself staring at Tommy's thick, dirty finger.

"Watch your mouth, kid," Uncle Tommy said seriously. There was a moment of stillness, then Tommy spoke to me without moving. "You got a score?"

I swallowed hard. "Yeah."

He leaned back and smoked. "All right. Tell me what kind of stuff."

I closed my eyes and thought about it and, to my horror, I heard Trim's voice lilting through the room.

"Sorry if I touched on a sore spot, Tom—literally."

I opened my eyes to a still life. Uncle Tommy was apparently staring at the floor, a beer in one hand and a cigarette in the other. Trim was grinning at him, his face bright red and his eyes watery. Dan was studying the table.

Tommy leaned forward.

Dan said without looking up "Uncle Tommy, lay off, okay?"

Tommy paused, then leaned back. "You don't know nothing about me, kid," he said quietly.

I jumped in. "We got computers, fax machines, copy machines, phones, radios, coffee makers, all the standard office shit."

"The phones on a voice mail system?"

"Yeah."

"Digital?"

"I think so."

He shook his head. "Can't use 'em. Forget the fucking phones. This stuff gonna be real hot?"

I shrugged. "Stolen, sure."

"No, you fucking moron," he said in the same tone of voice that was suddenly not pleasant, "I wanna know if I got to hide it and sit on it for a few fucking months or will it be clear to unload? You gonna be on the run?" He sighed in disgust. "What I wanna know, kid, is are you gonna be public enemy number one on this?"

"No," I said.

"How you know?"

"What?"

Uncle Tommy gave me the impression that he was keeping his temper by the smallest of possible margins. "What steps, *professor*, are you taking to make sure they don't suspect you. Jesus fucking Christ, you shitheads have a fucking plan, right?"

I cleared my throat. I wasn't enjoying this.

"Yeah."

Uncle Tommy leaned back. "Well? Let's hear it."

I opened my mouth to explain it to him, feeling like I was on some sort of warped job interview, but Dan held up his hand and I shut my mouth with a click. "Uncle Tommy," he said, and Tommy turned his head just slightly to indicate he was listening, "this isn't your problem. We need to know where you want the stuff, when, and how. Everything else is our end."

Tommy squinted his eyes up stubbornly. "Dan—"

"Come on, Uncle Tommy."

Uncle Tommy studied his nephew for a moment, then shrugged. "Okay, okay, I'll back off, okay? Jesus, I'm risking a lot, you know. You shitheads ain't professionals. I don't want to do time again, you know."

"I know," Dan said.

"Okay, then." He looked around the floor again, as if his eyes were searching for something. "You don't fucking know anything about me, kid."

We three desperados went out to dinner after Uncle Tommy had heaved himself out of the kitchen and down to the street. He'd given us an estimate of what our haul might be worth: thirty-five, maybe forty grand. It depended on a lot of things he didn't get very specific with, and he didn't seem happy about it. We went to El Torito and ordered margaritas to sit on top of our beers, burned more cigarettes in the no-smoking zone, and giddily reviewed our first brush with actual crime.

"Is planning a crime a crime?" Trim asked carefully. He was still jazzed from getting slapped around.

"Conspiracy to commit," Dan said heavily, "is."

"Are you sure?" I asked. "Hard to prove."

Dan shrugged drunkenly. "Hard to prove don't mean it ain't illegal."

Our waitress was a sassy, leggy brunette who tiredly welcomed us to El Torito while fidgeting around, looking for a pen. She glanced around and sighed.

"Sorry guys, you can't smoke here. I can—"

"Leave us alone, sister," Trim grumbled in a theatrical growl. "Or we'll burn the place down."

I snorted in shocked surprise, snuffing out my cigarette. "Ignore him. Have some goddamn courtesy, Trim."

Trim snorted back at me. "Sorry, sister," he said, putting out his own cigarette with a grin. She looked us over with tight lips and walked away. Trim immediately lit another cigarette.

I shook my head. "Man, you're a fucking asshole."

"Yeah," he said. "Hey, Dan, can we trust that Uncle of yours? He seemed a trifle excitable."

Dan was halfway to pie-eyed. He offered Trim his long, steady gaze that could be mistaken for a slow burn if you hadn't seen it before, which I had. It meant he was a little too drunk to think fast.

"What the fuck you expect?" he asked. "You were pretty goddamn rude."

"Thanks," Trim replied, "for calling me pretty."

Dan shook his head in disgust and sipped the blue thing in front of him. "We've got a month and a half. Dub, this is mostly your game right now. You up for it?"

The margaritas were refueling my system, and I was feeling expansive. "You betcha. All I gotta do is nail down a key card and we're set."

"Yeah. Set." Trim didn't sound convinced.

We ordered three Macho Combos and were disgusted, to a man, at the sight of so much refried beans. We ordered three more drinks, and by the time the check came we were toasting each other and feeling like a trio of walking hard-ons, ripping off the world.

Trim picked up the check, laughing.

"Holy shit," he said mildly, catching his breath. "We're gonna have to make this work just to finance this night."

5. Conversation II

The filthiest word you can utter in the presence of a woman is "cunt." Context doesn't really apply.

Trim liked the word because it was one of the few curses that hadn't lost its edge; it was one of the few things you could say in everyday conversation that would shut everybody up and cause a ruckus. You could tell everyone to fuck off and they just laughed, and *shithead* was almost a term of endearment amongst my friends. Nothing else had any air of darkness about it. Call someone a cunt, and you really stirred the shit up. Call a woman a cunt, and you had better be wearing some sort of protective clothing.

We had made a lot of decisions regarding our big caper, and once these things had been decided there was very little for us to actually do until some time went by. We had, for example, decided to catalogue what we would be stealing in advance, in order to give Uncle Tommy an accurate idea of how much storage space would be required, and also to make the actual heist as smooth as possible. I had the bright idea of just meeting them for lunch and walking around the office with them, introducing them to people, and they could make notes as they went. Trim thought this was absurdly simple and loved it. Dan thought it was dangerous to show all our faces around the scene of the eventual crime.

"They'll recognize us," he complained.

"Actually," I thought out loud, "that's probably good. This way when I bring you guys along at Christmas it won't seem so weird."

"Good point." Trim grinned.

Once this plan had been added to our growing masterpiece, though, there wasn't much to do about it. We had begun the waiting game, and our preferred mode of waiting was in a bar, with glasses warming in our hands. Unfortunately, the dark side of Trim's Theory of Diminishing Returns was beginning to rear its ugly head: we were spending way too much time together, and the strain of being nice to the same people all the time was beginning to show. To put it bluntly, we were running out of things to talk about, like a star collapsing in on itself for lack of gas to burn. A black hole was forming from which nothing could escape, and we were getting sucked into it against our wills—or my will, since Dan was generally too gassed to think that deeply about it, and Trim, well, Trim enjoyed gravity. He was waiting for the implosion with bated-breath.

I was brooding in Trim and Dan's living room, reading some of Trim's obscure books and just passing a Friday night. Trim was there, writing on the couch and occasionally trying lines out on me; I disliked them all and he was getting annoyed, which I thought was pretty goddamned immature. Dan was out somewhere, and all in all I was planning to hang around a few more hours and then go home for some sleep. The phone rang, and Trim told me to get it, because he was hiding from his less artistic friends.

Chick Parker had found Dan in Joe Odd's and had decided to track us all down for some drinks. Being a schmuck, I decided to go. Trim sat up.

"Where are we going?"

"Who invited you?"

He pulled on his boots. "They called my number, didn't they? Besides, I don't necessarily need an invite, in the abnormal situation that some less advanced individual fails to see the obvious benefits I bring to any social event."

And so we ended up in Joe Odd's Roost at ten o'clock. Trim immediately found a few cronies to beat backs with, and I found myself alone with Chick, who was apparently happy to see me. Naturally, I had nothing to say.

"What's wrong, Dub?"

I grinned like a loon. "Nothing."

Chick Parker was a smart girl, with the brightest eyes I'd ever seen; they shone and sparkled and more or less unmanned me. She was about to say something smart back to me about this obvious lie when Trim showed up and disaster struck.

He leaned between us, sweaty and snappy. "What are we talkin' about, huh?"

"Assholes," I said brightly.

Trim took that in good humor, smiling and settling down with us. Chick made room for him, but with a look toward me that suggested she'd rather be doing something else. I took this as an encouraging sign and tried to get rid of Trim, who was a classically difficult person to get rid of, since he patently didn't care what anyone thought of him. But I was pursuing the Holy Grail of the sensitive young man's life: the friend turned girlfriend. With that in my sights, I would have gladly gotten rid of my mother.

"Damien," she said carefully, using his real name because it bothered him, "we're having a private conversation here."

Trim grinned at me and nudged me in the ribs. "Told you we'd hook her for you."

I opened my mouth to tell him to fuck off.

"Fuck off." Chick beat me to it.

Trim winked at her and turned away. "No need to be a cunt about it, missy."

There was a moment of confusion on my part. One minute Chick was next to me, a nice, warm presence against my arm. Next, she had walked after Trim, grabbed him by the arm, spun him, and slapped him across the face wholeheartedly.

"You," she said quietly, "you never call me that."

Trim rubbed his cheek and studied her with that mad glint I'd come to have some affection for. He was still grinning. It was the second time in two weeks he'd been hit in the face, third time in a month. I think he was beginning to enjoy it.

A half-second before he reared to slap her back, I stepped forward, feeling his intention in some inexplicable way and meaning to make him eat it. I didn't have to. His hand went back, Chick's face went pale, and Dan stepped forward with all the broken-nose grace of a real scrapper and caught Trim's frail hand in his own meaty paw.

"Don't you fucking do it," Dan advised.

Trim stared at him, and the smile faded. "Oh, fucking hell," he muttered, and tore away from Dan, who let him go. Trim disappeared into the street, and the three of us looked at each other in that vague embarrassment that follows most violently awkward social situations. Dan shrugged, and Chick leaned over and planted one on his cheek. I was insanely jealous.

"Thanks, Dan."

He shrugged again, humorless. "You don't hit a girl," he said quietly, looking carefully at the floor. "Ever."

She smiled sunnily. "Your mom taught you well."

He glanced up and then down again. "Mom didn't teach me," he said, and turned to sit down, tense and blackened.

Chick looked after him. I stared at Chick, who was absolutely gorgeous in this mixture of pain and triumph. When she looked back at me, I turned away, ashamed.

"Wanna take a walk?" she asked me.

I managed enough cool to act unsurprised. "Sure."

"What's up with you three, anyway?"

We had lit cigarettes to ward off the chill of November. The city streets were teeming, but less so than during the day, and so seemed cozy.

"What'ya mean?"

She shrugged gracefully. "C'mon. Dan's drinking like a fish—or more of a fish than usual. Trim's usual pathos has turned a nasty shade of brown at the edges, and you just sort of show up. You used to be more there, Dub."

"I don't know," I said, and stopped.

She bumped me deliciously. "Come on, Dub. You three are like my best friends. What bizarre pagan ritual are you getting yourselves into this time?"

I slowed down a step, then immediately picked up the pace. "I didn't know we were your best friends," I said in disgust.

She was busy smoking. "Well, yeah."

"We're like the fucking Rat Pack," I said sourly, and laughed.

Now she was looking at me again. "Dub—"

"It's nothing," I said glibly, speeding up as she slowed down. I turned to walk backward, facing her as we moved. "We're just going through male menopause."

"Dub—"

I flicked my cigarette away. "Chick, I just said—"

"I heard you."

And that's where we left it.

When I got home, Trim was sitting on my building's front steps, staring at the sidewalk.

"You been talking about me all this time?" he asked the sidewalk.

I sat down next to him. "Nope."

"That's disappointing."

I nodded. "I know. But if it's any comfort, we do talk a lot about you at other times."

"I'm sorry about that, Dub."

"Don't apologize to me."

He stood up, and still stared at the sidewalk. "I just did. See you later."

I heard him walk off, and I went upstairs.

My apartment was tiny, filled with borrowed heirlooms. I couldn't afford anything, and I was rarely home long enough to gather enough inertia to clean, and the clutter and the dust and the alien possessions passed down from unseen friends and relatives and ancestors, it all clumps up and makes it hard to move, to breathe. I fought my way to the recliner and collapsed into it. I had a moment of sitting in the dark, listening to the dust settle, and then the phone rang.

I waited three rings. "Hello?"

Before she spoke, I thought about my crummy apartment, eating into every paycheck for the privilege of living in a shoebox, a coffin, a place you couldn't fit more than three people into even if they all held their breath. I thought about my crummy bar tab, and how I had to consider every cocktail weightily as if it would make or break me. I considered the fact that I was going to wake up in a few hours, put together spare change for the bus, eat fumes and rude commuters for a few hundred hours, and earn the small, useless salary they saw fit to award me. Based on my obvious charm and intellect. I thought about my credit cards, my car loan on a car that had stopped running months ago, my Mom, who I still owed thirteen hundred dollars. I thought of all these things.

And then I hung up on her.

6. Keeping It In the Family

Being a cubicle jockey in the city is the bottom rung of the ladder of power and success, but you are, at least, on the ladder. I worked on the 32nd floor of a huge office building that disappeared into the skies with a gasp and a wink at gravity, the elevators groaning with the impossible height, and the windows unopenable and dense. I had three walls, a computer, a phone, and a desk. Plus a million pieces of paper, arranged as delicately as could be. I also had them arranged on the floor, on my computer, and on my chair, although management frowned on all that and not a day went by that I didn't get shit for it. I was twenty-five, college educated, and getting paid to perform a skilled service, but my company seemed to feel that I lacked basic neatness, like a small child that couldn't stop spitting up.

But still, it was that phone, the voicemail, the computer, the business cards—all of it—that made me a human being in New York and not just another street person, another fucking tourist. I had a base to operate from, someplace people could call and leave messages for me, someplace to send faxes, to meet people, someplace I was included in. Walking the street I was acutely aware of having something, however small. I was not without means, as long as I had this fucking job.

And yet, it bothered me.

I walked the street and felt the heavy weight of Corporate America behind me, but I didn't like it. I was out of control and I didn't like the idea that if I got fired tomorrow (always a possibility with my attitude) I'd be a fucking tourist.

My cubicle was comically crowded. The walls were covered in photographs and memos, pinned up more or less at random, postcards, and greeting cards. I had pictures of Trim and Dan in some bar, giving me the finger, and pictures of Chick and other girlfriends, some I still talked to, some who were faded people I used to know. A birthday card from my mom, a couple of ribald e-mails I'd printed out. I had a bunch of plastic army men sitting on top of my computer, and six pairs of Converse Chucks underneath my desk. I had done all I could to deny the simple fact that I was a drone, a worker bee.

I picked up the phone and dialed my mom.

"Hello?"

"Hey, Mom."

"Hi! How are you?"

"Fine. What's up?"

"Nothing. Just making breakfast."

"Oh. Hey, do you have Frankie's number?"

"Your cousin Frank?"

"Yeah."

There was a suspicious pause.

"Phil—"

"Mom, I just gotta ask him some questions." My Mom never called me Dub, which I suddenly thought was strange.

"About what?"

I sighed in annoyance. "Mom, do you have his number?"

She sighed. "I have Aunt Carrie's number. I think Frank's staying with her right now."

"Go ahead."

She gave it to me, and I had to endure a short speech about cousin Frank's time in jail and how I shouldn't let the "glamour" of it all make me tag along with Frankie. It was very ironic that mom thought I was going to steal cars. I promised her I wouldn't, and that seemed to be good enough. I suffered through two more minutes about her garden, and then we hung up, leaving me to stare at the number I'd printed on my pad.

I dialed it, carefully.

"Hello? Aunt Carrie? It's Phil, yeah, Philly. Listen, uh, yeah, I'm still in New York. Hey, is, um, Mom's fine, she told me to have you call her. Her garden's fine. Yeah. Yeah. Uh huh. Well, um, is Frank around? Thanks."

I tapped a pencil against my pad.

"Frankie? It's your cousin Phil. Listen, I need a favor."

"You want me to do what?"

I didn't like the playful light in Trim's eyes, but I couldn't ask anyone else. Dan was my only other choice, anyway, and Dan and I had never been comfortable with each other. And recently he had been creeping me out, walking around half-crocked all the time and talking in grim monosyllables. Trim wasn't my best friend—I wasn't even sure I liked him much these days—but he was one of two people who knew I was a criminal, at heart. I needed him.

"I want you to come with me to talk to Frankie."

"Your younger cousin."

"By one year."

"You're afraid of your younger cousin."

I offered him my best pissed-off stare.

He waved me away with an irritable cigarette. "All right, all right. Why do you need a shotgun man to meet your younger cousin? I thought the Dublens were a peaceful folk?"

"Only until the booze hits us, and it hits us hard," I said. "No, Frank is going to steal us a van, so we can haul our stuff away."

He took me by the arm and walked me along the sidewalk. It was a crisp and sunny day and Thanksgiving wasn't far away. I wondered if I would ever have a free moment without Trim again.

"Fine, I'll go. Whatever. Maybe he'll punch me. You sure he can get us a van? Untraceable?"

"Untraceable? How the hell should I know? You've been watching those *Starsky and Hutch* reruns again. But we can't just rent a van from Budget and use it in a grand larceny, you moron. I figure at least if it's stolen it can't be traced to us on a paper trail."

This seemed like good logic, after all. Trim shrugged it off with a cavalier attitude that disturbed me.

"Cool. Everything is coming together. The rest seems to be up to you, huh?"

I offered him my *Cool Hand Luke* stare, which made me look rather unlike Paul Newman. "Maybe you ought to bring me up to speed on what, exactly, you bring to this party."

He slipped his arm around me and let the sun glint off his sunglasses. "Dub, besides enough info on you and Dan to put you both behind bars, I possess the one thing neither of you have in any amount: attitude."

I snorted. "Oh, you've got attitude, all right."

"Dub, m'boy, you need me because in pressure situations you need someone to do some fast talking and quick stepping. I'm the Bill Murray of our little group. I bring the razzle-dazzle."

"I think I'll concentrate on that part about you putting me in jail."

Trim clapped me on the back. "Whatever. When are we meeting your handsome rebel of a cousin?"

I looked at my watch. "Fifteen minutes. You ever hear of a bar called Millers?"

Trim stopped and stared at me. "What did you say Frankie did time for?"

I grinned. "Don't worry. I specified a place we wouldn't get killed in."

When we were kids, I went through a brief period where I idolized Frankie. He came to live with us for a few years when I was ten, and even though he was younger than me he had an attitude and a behavioral problem I couldn't compete with. Frankie could burp the alphabet and play with a butterfly knife at the age of nine. To me, he was the ultimate in cool.

Frankie and I went in different directions, however; he to junior rehab cum correctional facilities, me to mild academic success and eventual limp intellectual cronyism. By the time I was fifteen he regarded me as a slightly geeky and possibly homosexual relative of his, and while age had granted some small measure of respect Frankie still seemed to regard me as a younger relative, even though I had almost two years on him. Usually, it irritated me. Recent events, however, had made me think that maybe I should have hung out with Frankie more, and maybe taken part in the infamous Dublen Crime Spree, which is what sealed Frankie's place as black sheep of the family.

After he'd been with us for a few months (apparently casing our largely middle-class city neighborhood), Frankie hit upon a grand scheme that had apparently been handed down to him by young street hoodlums from the beginning of time. It was very simple: you got some of your young pals to distract grocery store owners while you robbed them blind.

Due to my innocent, slightly dimwitted demeanor (no doubt), I was Frankie's first choice as decoy. As dimwitted as I was, I could still sense that this unsavory scheme would bring me into Frankie's inner circle, which seemed like a high-rent district at the time. I was supposed to walk into a store with Frankie and his little hoodlum friends, veer off, and ask the proprietor as many cherubically idiotic questions as I could think of, while Frankie and his dumpling gang cleaned the poor guy out of Clark Bars and Super Pinkies.

I would have been good at it, too.

I was a stubborn child, however, and I was always getting beaten up (pretty badly, too) because I refused to back down. The harder you pushed me, the more you terrified me, the more incapable of speech or movement I became. So, when I say "stubborn" you understand that I mean "petrified." The two were often confused, and I have coasted on my childhood reputation for toughness ever since. When Frankie and his little hoodlum friends descended on me to intimidate me into being their decoy, my eyes narrowed, my legs locked, and my throat dried up. I silently resembled Jimmy Cagney, refusing (or inable) to respond even when they shoved me around. In disgust, they left me behind and went on to screw the whole thing up, getting caught after a week of giddy success. While they got off lightly due to their tender years, I know that Frankie always thought they would have gotten away with it if only I'd come along.

Contemplating this slice of nostalgia, I thought it ironic that I was now going to try and drag Frankie into one of my own lame-brained schemes. Trim and I found Millers without difficulty, slid into a booth in the rear, and ordered domestic beer on tap. Trim lit a cigarette, but I resisted.

Frankie was on time; it was his lunch hour, so he didn't have a lot of time to mess with. He was working straight at a friend's auto shop, rebuilding carbs and replacing mufflers, and so was greasy and darkened as he slid in across from me, next to Trim, who offered him his patently delerious smirk. Frankie did a double take on that, then obviously decided to leave it be, turning back to me.

Frankie was twenty-three but looked older to me. His hair was long and greasy and he had that naturally hard body that would eventually melt into fat, but not soon enough for my taste. He had fat Elvis sideburns and an insolent way of sitting that made me glad to have Trim and *his* idiotic bravado with me.

"Philly," Frankie said with a slight nod.

"Hey, Frank. Thanks for coming."

He grinned. "Since you're gonna buy me a couple of beers, I figure what the fuck."

"How are ya?"

"Hanging in. You?"

"Good. Good. Mom says hello."

"Yeah, how is Aunt Gretch?"

"Good. She putters, you know?"

He laughed. "Uh-huh."

I glanced at Trim, who was studying my cousin as if he were an interesting new species, and back at Frank. "I need you to get me a truck, Frankie."

He squinted at me. "What?"

"I need you to get me a truck."

He leaned back and fixed me with a canny stare. "I didn't go to college, Philly, so maybe you got a different meaning of the word 'get' than I do, huh?"

I flushed. "Okay. Steal, Frankie. I need you to steal a truck or a van for me."

Trim winked at me. "Ah. The New Honesty. I like it."

"Fuck off," I snapped.

"Keep the smart shit to yourself, paleface," Frankie snapped on top of me. We glanced at each other, and for a second we were just Dublens, the both of us.

Frankie stared at Trim for a moment, giving him his best hardass look. Trim seemed not to notice, having found something fascinating about his cigarette. He was smirking, though, and I knew we hadn't heard the last from the idiot. Frank looked back at me.

"Why, Philly?"

I shook my head. "Frankie, I just need a truck, okay?"

He shook *his* head, and I wondered if we looked alike at that moment, with the same vague genetic code waltzing through our veins. "Uh-uh, cuz. I need to know. You think I get into these conversations for fun? You don't talk to me for two years, Philly, except at—"

I stuck a finger in his face. "If you're gonna tell me you're hurt, that is the biggest line of bullshit, Frank. You telling me you were—"

"Philly, I—"

"And stop calling me Philly, goddamn it! I'm twenty-five fucking—"

We both stopped mid-sentence and leaned back to glare at each other. Trim snickered. "We've been having great luck with these family reunions, huh, Dub?"

Frank and I looked at each other, and I sighed. "I've got an opportunity, Frankie, and I need a truck to haul stuff, one that can't be traced back to me." I winced. As expected, Frankie laughed.

"Jesus, Philly, you're fucking ripping someone off?"

"We ain't going cruisin' for chicks," Trim growled in mock machismo.

"Him I don't like," Frankie said, leaning back expansively. "But, I need to know details."

I threw my hands up. "Everybody needs a fucking novel."

That night I showed up at Rue's Morgue to hear Trim read a poem at the open mike, and ended up sitting with a friend of his named Karyn with a "y" who had bad teeth and worse manners, who I chased away with insults and cigarette smoke. Trim was well-known at the Rue's open mike events, and got booed enthusiastically when he took the stage and announced that his poem was entitled "IN LOVE WITH CHICK." Our eyes met, and he winked, and I knew that I hated the bastard. The poem was bizarre and filled with German words, which drove the crowd into a frenzy. At one point, during a stanza which (I gathered) had something to do with sipping from the stagnant toilet water of cunnilingus, I resisted the urge to shout something at him.

Walking home with Trim, I reminded him about his rule of never using the word 'love' in his poems, and he replied that it hadn't been *in* the poem, it had been in the *title* of the poem, natch. I gave up on that and asked him about the German.

"I don't speak a word of it," he said. "Those morons sure loved it though, huh? They think German equals death equals good fucking poetry."

And just like that, I forgave him, and we walked home in companionable silence.

7. MINUTIAE

IT TOOK ME JUST ONE DAY to become irritated with Trim again.
I came home from work to find thirteen messages from
Trim on my machine, all of them apparently misdials.

Sandwiched between them was a hesitant call from Chick
Parker, asking me to give her a call if I wanted to get a cup
of coffee after her late shift at the bar that night. She didn't
sound very hopeful about the prospect. At the end of
Trim's ridiculous struggle with coherency was a message
from Dan, who had quit his temp job a few days before
and had been hanging out in Old Man Bars ever since.

Old Man Bars described the sort of watering holes that
had a specific, atrophying, and terminal group of customers:
old men spending pension checks. You could walk into
these places at any time of day or night and find the same
ten or twelve old men sitting around nursing drinks, cigarettes, and opinions. No one in them was ever under fifty,
and no one in there thought it odd if you ordered a bourbon with water back at one in the afternoon. Or ten in
the morning.

Invariably, these places shared other qualities: nonstop
Sinatra in the air, pinball machines, a lack of cable TV,
and a complete dislike of anyone under fifty. Dan was
twenty-seven years old, but he had nothing better to do,

and over the past week I'd gotten used to finding him drunk at four in the afternoon, ready for a nap before a grim dinner with Trim or me. Overnight, Dan had turned into an old man, a Grifter. I didn't enjoy talking to Dan any more. All he talked about was the plan and how bored he was.

"Dub, it's Dan. Gimme a call at Leary's when you get in, okay? I'm here all day, I think. If not, try me at home."

It was the same fucking message he left practically every day. He wanted to do dinner. I couldn't wait for a few more weeks to pass by, and we would actually start to *work*.

On Wednesday I went on a date with Christine, an acquaintance of my friend Margaret. Margaret firmly believes in matchmaking, despite her near-zero success rate. It had worked out once, and that one time had become her Holy Grail, her talisman. Usually I have the good sense to refuse her offers, but I was tired—tired of thinking about nothing but this scheme, of hanging out with Trim and Dan, tired of avoiding Chick. I found myself wanting to just hang out and flirt, have a few drinks with someone not armed with Trim's withering bullshit or Dan's freezing ennui. So I threw caution to the wind and said sure, and Margaret gave me Christine's number.

Christine, I remembered, was a cute, bubbly girl, olive-skinned and dark-haired, with a nice rack and a dainty way that I usually found annoying. I didn't like girls who acted girly, as a rule; I preferred women who could curse and wrestle and tell off-color jokes. Christine, I recalled, was the sort who held fast to the concept that there were certain things a lady did not do. Still, she was attractive, she was interested, and I suspected she was not smart enough to pick up on the very real boredom pervading my every interaction these days.

I hadn't been on a date in a long, long time. It's funny how twenty-five sneaks up on you and suddenly things that seemed so easy a few short years ago are so arcane, so unbelievably impossible. I called Christine and found that I had absolutely no small talk left in me. Not only didn't I have any words for her, but I didn't even have the decency-slash-energy to invent some. Thank goodness Christine was a talker, and filled in the blank spots with a cheerful tirade about her day, how terrible it had been at work, and how pleased she was that someone was coming to the rescue and buying her a drink. I said how about seven and she said fine.

I sat and stared at the phone for a moment, completely unsure what to do next. I thought back to my last first date, and to my horror realized it had been five years ago, with Arlene Zim. Trim used to call her "The Amazing Zim" with his best sarcastic wink, since she had been one of the dullest people I'd ever known. That had been back in college, which meant all I'd had to do was bring her to one of the seven thousand parties going on off campus, get her liquored up, back off after a spirited attempt at sex before I became too creepy, and just like that it was a success. Now I was twenty-five, and I had a bad feeling that the rules had changed, that maybe I was supposed to do something impressive, something romantic.

I broke out in a sweat.

I wondered what I'd been doing these past few years. I didn't remember joining a monastery, and I certainly hadn't been suddenly gay; I knew plenty of girls and had even slept with a few in the past five years, although not, admittedly, within the past two. Two years ago I had started losing steam for endless nights in bars and prowling around the city looking for open diners, and I'd also met Chick, which somehow had translated into me not caring so much anymore.

I put on a jacket and tie, shaved, splashed some cologne on, and showed up five minutes early, smoking to calm myself. Christine lived in a brownstone that had seen better days, with two roommates who were eating ice cream and watching TV, and who didn't even look up at me while I waited. She wore a short skirt that showed a lot of stockinged leg and a provocative sweater unbuttoned at the top to show a bit of smooth chest. Her hair was up in a casual way that must have taken some doing, and her face was lightly made up. She smelled wonderful.

I was struck, suddenly, with the apparently ridiculous idea that maybe I was, after all, desirable. That maybe this girl thought I was a good catch. The idea, alien as it was, kept me in good spirits for a while.

We went to an upscale bar on Sixth Avenue called Magoo's, the sort of place that charged six dollars for a mixed drink and thought happy hour meant turning on the jukebox. I knew if I took her to one of my usual dollar beer haunts we'd all be in trouble. I ordered a whiskey sour and bought her a gin and tonic, and sat back to listen to her chatter on about her day. She was a chatterer, the sort of person to whom silence equaled death. I bought us a second round, and it just made her chatter more. For the third round, we moved to a table, and I noticed that Christine couldn't hold her liquor all that well: she was already flushed and a little slurry, and when her leg rubbed up against mine, it was definitely on purpose. I knew with some vague male power that one more drink and the night would have an interesting ending. I thought about it for a few minutes while she scooted closer to me in order to whisper some intimate detail to me, and then asked her if she wanted another. She did and giggled.

On my way to the bar, feeling unscrupulous, I somehow got lost and found myself at a pay phone.

"Hello?"

"Hey."

"Dub?" Chick was hard to hear in the noise of the bar, subdued as it was. "What's up?"

"I'm on a date."

There was a contemplative silence. "Well, hey—that's great. Why are you calling me, then?"

"I dunno, I guess I just . . . I just wanted to say hi. I just wanted to talk to you."

"It's been a while, Dub. Where've you been?"

"Ah, well . . . avoiding you, actually."

"No duh, Dub, you aren't exactly subtle. Why?"

I closed my eyes. "Doesn't matter. I'm—oh, hell—I'm sorry, Chick. I really am."

She sighed. "You know, Dub, when we talk like this maybe you ought to call me Adrian."

"Adrian? Where'd Chick come from?"

"My Dad wasn't real advanced when it came to women. He was a little disappointed when he didn't get a son, and he always called me 'the chick.'"

I chuckled. "I never knew that."

She laughed back. "I never told you."

I looked around. "I think I should get back to my date."

"I guess. You're a weird guy, Dub."

"Maybe you should call me Phil."

"Nah. Good-bye, Dub."
"Good-bye."

I stopped by the bar for our drinks and ordered an extra shot of bourbon for myself, either seeking the cold comfort of impotence or trying for a fire in the belly. I wasn't sure.

After two more rounds, Christine's chatter had become intriguing, and after one more I found I couldn't hear her very well and had to keep leaning in toward her to hear better. When she started nibbling on my ear every time I did this, I practically went deaf. I certainly couldn't tell you what we talked about.

When we'd decided to go home, I excused myself to the bathroom one final time. Standing in front of the mirror, ignoring the guys jostling for toilet space behind me, I studied my pasty, flushed face and decided the whole evening had been a big mistake, that I was standing on a precipice, and down at the bottom of the chasm was the next morning. I tightened my belt and went out to walk her home, filled with pure purpose and resignation.

It was a toss-up as to which one of us was the drunker; certainly she found it difficult to walk a straight line and spent the twenty-minute walk to her apartment a pleasant presence against my side, making us both walk a crazy zig-zag up the sidewalk, but I wasn't much better. She chattered on and on as we walked, a warm stream of words I let coast over my aerodynamic chassis, nodding and murmuring in the appropriate places to create the illusion of attention. When we reached her building, I had to stop her and point the fact out to her, which made her giggle, burying her face in my chest and gripping my jacket lapels forcefully.

When the giggles passed she looked up at me. "Will you come up?"

I smiled what I believe was the most insincere smile of my generally sincerity-challenged life. "No. That wouldn't be a good idea," I said softly. I didn't believe a word of it myself, and with her pressed against me as she was my erection was beginning to argue the point too, joining in with my Libido and my Sense of Injustice, all filibustering my internal dialogue, blocking my attempt to reclarify the arguments against fucking Christine.

A pretty frown formed on her face. "No?" She slid her arms around me.

My vision swam. Still, I have unplumbed reserves of paranoia and fear when it comes to women and sex, and I managed to shake my head with another gentle smile. "No."

She looked down into my chest again. "At least walk me up? Some of the hall lights are out. It's dark."

Dimly, in the background, I could hear my Libido and Sense of Injustice laughing at me.

Every single hall light I observed was in perfect working order as we ascended three flights of stairs in a weird jellied silence, me with my eyes scrupulously on the steps instead of on her ass. At her door she turned to face me, leaning against the jamb, and reached out to play with my jacket lapels.

"Sure you won't come in?" she asked quietly, and pulled me forward with disturbing force.

She was a terrible kisser, and for a moment my Sense of Injustice and Libido were cowed by a sudden uprising of what for want of a better term I'll call my Good Sense. The initial exploratory peck on the lips was nice and sweet, the half-open melt-against-each-other followup was promising. But just as I slid my arms around her and molded her against me, eliciting a little girlish grunt, she opened wide and pushed her tongue into my mouth, thrashing it about with wild abandon and zero finesse. My eyes popped open in startled fear, but thankfully hers were glued shut.

"You're not really going home?" she said when we parted for air.

I knew I wasn't, somewhere, but on the surface I was still kidding myself. "I don't want to, but I should."

She kissed me again, a series of light pecks on my lips, nice. "You're not going home."

I wasn't going home.

Phase Two of my Seminar on Bullshitting Yourself was when I decided that while I wasn't going home, there was no way I was going to have sex with her. We unlocked the door and slipped inside the place trying to walk, kiss, and laugh all at once. We found one of Christine's roommates sitting up with a bowl of ice cream, reruns of *The Honeymooners*, and a bong the size of a baseball bat. The roommate just glanced at us with reddened eyes, smiled, and went back to the TV. Christine and I burst out laughing, and she grabbed my hand and led me to her room.

The game plan I'd negotiated with my Libido and Sense of Injustice was that I'd make out with her, but I wouldn't screw her, because that would be disaster. Besides, for some reason I kept thinking about Chick Parker, and that was pretty worrisome. I think I had a fighting chance, too, when I got a good look at her room in the soft yellow light of her Minnie Mouse table lamp.

I froze for a moment, finding myself regarded by a thousand or so sewn-on eyeballs, the largest collection of stuffed animals I'd ever seen in my life, all lined up on shelves on every wall of the room like an audience. I ran a hand over my sweaty face, frozen in shock, and for the first time in about two hours I felt my erection diminishing.

Then Christine jumped me.

She pushed my jacket off and pulled me to the bed by my belt. The bed had several favored stuffed creatures lined up on it, and I was minorly encouraged when she swept them onto the ground without a care. Thinking back, if she'd spoken to them, introduced me to them, or in any way indicated she thought they were sentient I would have shook her hand and walked away, whistling "Show Me the Way to Go Home" without regrets. She didn't, though. She jammed her tongue back in my mouth like she was going to suck my fillings out and began struggling to undo my belt. At that moment my higher mental functions flat-lined, leaving me with only my Libido and Sense of Injustice, which were toasting champagne and doing belly-slams in celebration.

The rest of it was somehow typical, in a way. She undid my belt and tentatively caressed me through my BVDs (this moment being the first time in the whole process it occurred to me to be concerned about the state of my underwear: happily, relatively new) and I, as usual, got ticklish. I got her blouse off with a modicum of skill and style, found her smooth shoulders irresistible, then took my eyes off the road for a fatal moment and lost control of her red satin bra. She cooed in my ear as I began working on the clasp, unseen and incomprehensible.

Into minute two of this futile attempt, I thought to my-self, *I bet Dan does this in his fucking sleep.*

When she leaned away from me with an amused and

flushed expression and unclasped it with a practiced move, I smiled and shrugged, and she giggled again, slipping the garment off shyly. She assumed a seductive expression and began tugging my pants down. Women always seem to think that giving a little head is the most erotic thing they can do. They're almost always wrong, but they make a big production out of it anyway.

I'm pretty ticklish, unfortunately, and as she was poised to engulf me she glanced up with a look of momentary concern. "You're not, like, a hair trigger, are you?" she whispered earnestly. I let my head sag back onto her pillows and barked a laugh, thinking that my dignity was quickly becoming an endangered species.

Once we got to the actual fornication, however, there was a subtle shift in the wind, and Christine, who up till the actual mounting had been pretty energetic, enthusiastic, and, plainly, mobile, decided her work here was done and lay back with her arms at her sides and her big eyes fixed directly on my sweating, most probably unattractive face. From this moment on, she did almost nothing aside from watch me with her spooky, *Village of the Damned* eyes as I humped away. I began to feel more and more like a bug climbing up her leg, oblivious and about to be crushed.

Now, I'm not one of those guys who requires a huge show of approval, and actually the leg-kicking scream-out-louders often make me suspicious of a con in the works, but I like a bare minimum of acknowledgment, the equivalent of a pat on the back and a chipper "Good show, chap!" is all I ask. Her lying there with her legs locked behind me and those dead orbs staring up at me was giving me the willies, which was seriously impeding my increasing desire to just get the fiasco over with.

When it was over, she got up immediately and went to the bathroom, returning in an oversized T-shirt and the scent of mouthwash to snuggle next to me. I lay there in the dark, feeling my sweat dry and my heart return to normal, saying nothing. When her breathing lengthened and deepened, I got up slowly and found my pants, slipping out into the living room to put them on and make sure I had all my possessions. I already felt like the biggest prick in the universe, and finding one of Christine's roommates still sitting on the couch, regarding me with stoned indifference didn't help.

I stood for a moment in my underwear. "Hi," I said.

She shook her head slowly. "I thought someone was killing an animal in there. Was that you?"

Slowly, I threaded one leg and then the other into my pants. It certainly wasn't the Mute in there. I said, "I guess it was."

As I slipped out of the apartment, I realized that while my Libido was gone, my Sense of Injustice had doubled in size.

At three in the morning, I found myself in the last place I wanted to be: an Old Man Bar with Dan, who was so drunk he could barely speak. I called Christine's number from the pay phone in the back and left her an apologetic and thoroughly wretched message concerning how much fun I'd had and how I'd call her soon and we'd go out again, knowing full well how I sounded. Completely depressed, I joined the waxy-eyed Dan at the bar. He grinned at me with wall-eyed charm.

"I'm an asshole," I said simply.

Charlie, the aged bartender with no front teeth, glanced up at me and seemed to be telepathically saying *you got that right, shithead.* Dan was having trouble keeping his eyes open.

"You ever want to just go back and make one decision differently?"

Dan nodded, and almost slipped off his stool.

I rubbed my eyes. "I got like thirty of them tonight alone."

He made three tries at grabbing his glass and missed.

I closed my eyes for a moment and thought about Chick. A sick feeling materialized in the pit of my stomach. I shook my head. "Such an asshole."

When I opened my eyes, Dan was face down on the bar. I raised an eyebrow and glanced up at Charlie. "Wanna call us a cab?"

He just shook his head. "No."

I winked. "Thanks."

On Saturday, Trim and I went food shopping at the local A&P, each of us looking to stay alive for a few more days. Shopping, as a bachelor, is a bizarre and unnecessarily complex event: it requires much too much planning and hard work, for something that really ought to be simple, since it's so essential.

The place was packed. We outran a pair of elderly women for the last available cart, and waltzed into the heated interior of the store with a nasty strut and a list. Mine had about a dozen things on it, the usual coffee, milk, eggs, bread, yadda yadda. Trim's list had just one thing on it: single mothers.

Trim was far from the effete artist with delicate hands;

he was as much the sexual predator as the rest of us. His Theory of Diminishing Returns, however, precluded putting any kind of real effort into the pursuit of the Beast with Two Backs, and in Trim's dim and rather oddly angled little world single mothers were the easiest prey there was.

"You see," he once explained (in painful detail, unwanted detail, detail inspired by a night of drinking Everclear shots) "these chicks get knocked up, usually pretty young—nineteen, eighteen—and they spend the next few years in this turmoil of family problems, legal and financial difficulties, not to mention making sure their kids are healthy and get a good start. Suddenly, they're twenty-five and they're lonely, bored, horny, you name it. They want to get out there and have a good time, you know? But most guys won't touch 'em, because the kids scare them away. They fear the commitment. These chicks are easy targets for a sensitive guy with puppy-dog eyes. You date 'em a few times and they're so fucking happy you're sticking around, they'll roll over in no time."

The key to his plan, of course, was the immense store of insincere charm Trim had been born with. Rationed out over the years, he still had plenty left. The only defense I can offer of Trim and this rather mangy and ignoble plot to steal hope from single mothers' hearts through cheap, heartless sex, is that I don't think he ever succeeded at it.

The supermarket, of course, was a mecca for mothers of all stripes, so it only stood to reason that a few of the younger ones were unmarried. Trim tried to convince me to let him have the cart alone, fearing we might be taken for a gay couple, but I refused. I needed groceries.

We did a slow, rhythmic cha-cha up and down the aisles, snatching what we could from the shelves. I stayed clear of the coupon specials and one-day sales, knowing that every cub scout–breeding bitch in her casuals would be snarling around the sale items. Trim leered at them all, until the security guard left the carts unguarded outside to tail us grimly. I shopped like a typical bachelor, more concerned with cookies and burritos than with nutrition and long life. We took turns pushing the cart to insane speeds and jumping on, riding it until we crashed into the single mothers as a way of breaking the ice. After an hour, my cart was piled high with the basic building blocks of life: microwave dinners, coffee, cookies, and cheese.

I noticed that Trim had slipped some of his own groceries in, probably in the vain hope that I would pay for them unknowingly. I paid for them anyway. Everyone's got to eat, after all.

Standing at the checkout, Trim looked around cheerfully and leaned in close to me. "Hey, security here is a joke. Think this place keeps much cash in the safe?"

I wasn't amused.

On Sunday I found myself talking baseball with Dan and a guy named Norman at an Old Man Bar called Aprici's. A good way to predict whether a bar will be an Old Man Bar or a young man's place is to note the name. Old Man Bars are invariably named for their owners, or former owners, and are almost always Italian or Irish. The younger bars have names that have nothing to do with any of those things, and which often reflect the bizarre and unbalanced minds of the people who think owning a bar is a good way to retire. My theory on this: we kids just plain don't have anything left to talk about, and if it weren't for strange bar names, millions of first dates would never get past the stare-and-sweat stage.

Norman, whose last sober day had been circa 1965, was telling us that Mickey Mantle had been the greatest center fielder to ever play the game. I suspected that his allegiance to the Mick had something to do with their shared love of Wild Turkey on the rocks, and Dan, who had maybe seen one baseball game in his life, took the position that baseball sucked. In my experience, old drunken codgers always talked about Mickey Mantle as if he had been the only player, ever.

I'd never seen Mantle play, except in grainy footage and in my imagination, reading about him. I was more impressed with his sheer wastage of talent. I'd seen a lot of baseball, though, and it was my opinion that if Mickey Mantle had played in the modern day he would have looked old and tired against Pedro Martinez, just like everyone looked old and tired. This sent Norman into a spitting rage. I ignored him. Pedro Martinez had what I liked to call *The Look*: that drop-dead stare that froze hitters in their tracks. Steve Carlton had it, and Dwight Gooden had it before he'd gotten all goofy on drugs. In the films I'd seen, Bob Gibson had invented it.

When I was a kid, I played little league, badly. I'd always been amazed and fascinated by the nuance of baseball, the small stuff that happened fast and that no one who was not already a student of the game noticed. Every time Dan complained of how dull baseball was, I only shook my head: he just wasn't paying attention. Flashy sports like football were his style. A great at-bat was poetry, to me, and I'd always been tortured by the fact that while I could sit at home and see every fucking detail of the game, know every move, every fucking thought that went through their minds, put me in the batters box or at first base and I went numb, it all left me. I'd struck out forty-seven times in my little league career, and I remember every one. Every pitch. Every swing, the exact moment when I realized I'd fucked it up again—burned in, unforgettable.

Juan Gonzalez once said that baseball was a game of suffering, but baseball was beautiful. You either got that or you didn't.

I was having dinner with Mom that night, and I came very close to telling her all about our plot.

This wasn't out of any misplaced sentiment, or because I viewed Mom as a close confidant; my mother had become something of an icon to me, this person I owed so much to and who took such an interest in me despite the fact that I never understood why. She was inexplicable to me. Very simply, I found myself wanting to tell her because I couldn't think of anything else to say.

This had gotten me into trouble before. It was maddening, to sit across from your mother at her table and have nothing to say. On a few occasions I had let that madness carry me away, and the results had been eye-opening. I was older and wiser, however, and I bit my tongue this time. I could endure an uncomfortable silence or two like a man, I figured, and not have to explain to Trim and Dan why my own mother had turned us in, or perhaps simply forbade me to play with them any more.

Instead, I deflected.

"I'm a little worried about Dan," I announced to the yellowed wallpaper of the kitchen. My house was depressing these days, and had been for years. Homes get that way when you're just marking time.

"Hmmmn?" she asked. She was doing the crossword puzzle in the paper, leaning over so her bifocals could help.

"He's drinking too much."

Mom had been raised in a different set of decades. She shrugged. "He's young."

"He's my age. Should I start boozing it up?"

She glanced at me. "You know how to handle yourself."

"I'm afraid Dan doesn't, anymore."

That was how to get a point across—you had to find out what she was talking about and put it that way. She gave me a canny squint and asked "How bad is it?"

I shrugged. "Every day, every night. He looks like hell; he isn't even looking for a job anymore. It's almost like he's—"

I stopped. I'd been about to say *waiting for the caper.*

"Like he's what?"

"Waiting for something to happen. Marking time."

She nodded. "A lot of men mark time that way. Have you said anything to him?"

I shrugged. "Dan's not a talker, Mom."

"They never are."

We sat in silence then, for a while.

I left Mom's house late that night, because I'd fallen asleep on the couch watching football, and took a walk around the old neighborhood to see what might have changed since the last time I'd paid any attention to it. I found Pershing Field, the old park I'd played Little League in all those years ago, and wandered into it, breathing the cold air and wondering when they'd put in all the lights. The place was so bright and shadowless it might as well have been day.

I was mugged, once, in that park. The idea that it was so safe now saddened me, a little.

I found the old field and pushed myself against the chain-link fence, watching my breath steam. I was underdressed and shivering, and I remembered how I hated that field, how I dreaded my games, standing so futile in left field, or "left out" as it's known to anyone familiar with Little League.

Thirteen years later, I was a tired kid who smoked too much to play ball anymore, working a nothing job, with cynical, boozy friends, contemplating a small heist just to feel like I had choices. I didn't know how it'd happened.

"Hey."

I turned a little, and saw a cop coming my way, shining a flashlight in my face. I squinted at him.

"What are you doing here?"

I turned around completely. "Nothing much, I guess. Why?"

He was only a few feet away, and the fucking light was still in my face. I held out a hand to block it, and the bastard shifted it up a little to keep it in my eyes. "The park is closed, sir. I'll have to ask you to leave."

"Closed?" I asked. "Since when do they close a park?"

"Since about five years ago, sir. Let's go."

I started to walk, and he followed me. "Seems a little crazy, closing a park, if you ask me."

"I didn't," he said. I didn't like him much. "But if you'd been mugged here you might be singing a different tune."

I laughed. "I got mugged here four times before I was

sixteen, man. Doesn't stop me from taking a walk here sometimes. You start treating people like criminals and fools, and pretty soon we start acting like it."

"Jesus Christ," he muttered. "Just take a hike, buddy."

I couldn't catch a break.

8. THE DAME

HER NAME WAS DAME ANN MILLER, believe it or not, and she was going to be our stooge.

It was a month before the Christmas party, and I had Dan and Trim come by the office early for lunch to get a gander at the place, and to meet the people I worked with. This way, our logic went, when Dan and Trim showed up at the party bar excursion they wouldn't be strangers. They would also get a chance to meet Dame, and approve her as my stooge.

I was loving the word "stooge."

Dame Ann would tell you within five minutes of meeting you that her father had called her Dame because he knew, rather vaguely, that in England it was a title awarded you, and he wanted his little girl to be special. I don't think the poor confused bastard really knew what he was talking about, and the result was poor Dame, who had a remarkable name she could never live up to.

I worked in one of those big midtown buildings that had a huge empty lobby that was basically just an impressive waste of space, the builders' way of saying that they were so fucking rich they could afford to have this huge room filled with nothing, a room that would cost most of us thousands a month to rent. They usually had a couple of useless rentacops roaming the place, more interested in lunch than anything else. And it was packed with the sort of cookie-cutter business-degree stuffed shirt morons that made you want to gnaw your own limbs off to escape from. They all wore the same slate-gray suits and had the same Norman Rockwell haircuts, they carried the same tired briefcases and wore the same wingtip leather shoes. They had more fucking stuff than I could afford to buy in my entire lifetime: raincoats, overcoats, umbrellas, watches, rings, sunglasses, hats, briefcases, overnight bags, boots, shoes, whole *outfits* of clothes meant for minutely specific purposes. It boggled my mind, how you could own all that crap and not go mad. Me, I had three pairs of jeans and two pairs of dress pants, a couple of T-shirts and a couple of button-downs, a pair of Chucks, and a pair of soft leather loafers. These clothes got me through every situation, every climate, every moment. I had nothing, and I *still* lost track of socks.

Needless to say, I hated the place, more so because I knew somehow that I was in danger of becoming one of them. I was doing a pretty terrible job, but I was well-liked and not completely incompetent, and banking on the Peter Principle, I was likely to eventually find myself in a position I could not easily be fired from. And that kind of static security, not to mention the minor salary that came with it, made it easy to start buying things. And before you knew it, you were an old-timer, wearing a slate-gray suit.

As it was, a pack of cigarettes or a third round of drinks were my big purchases, to be agonized over, since the three bucks could be spent better elsewhere. I liked it that way.

Dan didn't have to take off work, since he was unemployed and loving it, and getting a day off from a video store wasn't the hell it used to be for Trim, so neither of them had much trouble showing up at the front desk at eleven-thirty in the morning. They were greeted suspiciously by the white-haired Dame, who obviously didn't think they belonged in *her* building, dressed as they were. She buzzed me and whispered into the phone, and I ruined her day by saying I'd be right out.

She watched me emerge from the office and shake their hands, laughing at some obscene joke Trim made as I appeared. I felt her eyes on me, disapproving, questioning, and I turned to her with the biggest shit-eating grin I could muster.

"Damien," I boomed heartily. "Dan, I'd like you to meet Dame Ann Miller, our receptionist."

Trim smiled and extended his hand. She was reaching for it with a wide, delighted smile of her own (the slate-gray suits I worked with rarely acknowledged Dame to any of their clients or friends) when he said "So, you're the blue-haired damsel our boy's been pining for in the bathroom every night! My goodness, Dame, for *hours* I mean!"

At first her return smile was vacant with polite cheer. Then it turned yellow and retreated, leaving her sitting there looking at Trim's hand in hers as if it were some sort of insect.

"She's perfect!" Trim chortled. I plucked the unlit cigarette from his mouth as he searched for matches.

"Can't smoke in here, hoss."

He made a face. "Fascists."

"She *is* perfect," Dan agreed. I wasn't used to hearing

him speak soberly anymore; it was kind of nice. "It's perfect that she's the receptionist."

"Yeah?" I asked.

We had stopped outside the door that led to my area, and I was poised to slide my keycard through the little slot.

"People always think receptionists are dumb and lazy," Dan said rather excitedly, as if his body were reveling in being dry. "Otherwise, these idiots think, why would they be receptionists? They're viciously polite to them, really ugly nice to them, but deep down they treat them like lower castes. Subconsciously, Dub, everyone here will roll their eyes when she complains she lost her card, and think *oh jesus poor Dame she can't even do simple things.*"

He was right. I punched in my code, and the door popped open with military efficiency. I led them to my cubicle. Trim sat down in my chair.

"Yuck. Get some walls, natch: this is unseemly."

"Easy as pie. First I have to reverse two years of my bad reputation. Then I have to actually learn my job."

Dan was looking around hungrily. "Dub, there might be more here than we expected, huh?"

I shrugged. "I doubt it. We shouldn't talk about it in public, though, huh? I'll give you the grand tour; just keep your mouths shut and don't steal any fucking staplers, okay?"

Dan nodded. "Okay, Chief, it's your deal." He put a manly hand on my shoulder and patted me, and it occurred to me that I would never be a fully accredited *guy*. Guys like Dan would always view me as a geek of sorts. That's why they called me things like *chief.*

Trim spun around in my chair. "Yikes. How do you keep from killing yourself in this box?"

"I drink," I said. "Come on, meet the office. And keep your eyes open, okay?"

Dan put a hand on my shoulder. "You know what?"

I regarded him, the sharp angles of his face, the bright green of his eyes, regarding me back with the amazing, dulled intelligence I'd taken for granted for years. "What?"

"This is the first step," he said slowly. "Once we give Uncle Tommy all the details tonight, we'll be committed. Tom's family, but if we make him pay out money and pull in favors, I can't guarantee he wouldn't kill us if we welsh."

There was a moment of quiet. I watched my screen saver, which made the sentence *You wouldn't know crazy if Charles Manson was eating Fruit Loops on your front porch* scroll across the screen over and over. I contemplated the wisdom of that statement, then Trim opened his mouth.

"*You* ought to be committed, Saucy," he said. "Let's go. Poppa needs a new pair of shoes."

My coworkers were a horny and suspicious lot, endlessly pursuing each other in boozy office flirtations that were wilted by immense paranoia right out of the gate. They were the sort of relationships wherein I had once been asked, in complete seriousness, what some girl had meant by "We should go out sometime, give me a call."

The only thing sadder, I thought, was the fact that I'd actually had to think a moment before responding.

The reactions to Trim and Dan were diverse; Dan caught the girls' eyes as a free-standing single male with no obvious physical deformities, and Trim didn't attract anyone at all until he opened his mouth, at which point Trim's ancient and sentient dark charm reared up to fill the floor. He played a game he and I had invented back at cock-jock frat parties we'd snuck into back in school: The Lying Game. The trick was, you made up new lies to tell every new person you met—the grander the better. If you made it through the night without getting caught in an outright lie, you won. If we both won, we bought each other breakfast.

Trim had never lost. I lost rarely, but Trim *never* lost.

He told Darlene in subscriptions that he was homosexual and had met me when trying to purchase sex from me one night in a bar, that when I'd gotten angry he'd gotten embarrassed and bought me a drink to apologize, and friendship bloomed. She seemed to think this was sweet.

He told Alex, the sixty-year-old grump in charge of the mail room, that he had always dreamed of working in publishing, that he was quitting his job as a bike messenger to do so, and that I had agreed to give him a tour of the place for inspiration. And that his name was Dexter. I almost laughed out loud.

By the time we'd made the rounds of the office, Trim had given out so many names, occupations, and character tics, *I* was confused. I walked them into the elevators, laughing. Between floors twelve and eleven, Dan pressed the STOP button. The alarm began ringing, loudly.

"What's up, amigo?" I asked, trying to stay cool. The alarm made me nervous. The elevator phone began to ring, too, but Dan leaned against it as if he suspected we might have an urge to answer it, and maybe confess.

"I just wanted to see what would happen. The more we know about your building, man, the better off we are. Try and open the doors."

I looked at Trim, who shrugged. "Better do what the big man says, palooka, or we might all end up taking the dirt nap."

"Fuck you," Dan said placidly. Sober, Dan was still a saint.

"Where'd you hear that? A movie?" I asked.

"Listen," Dan interrupted, "try the doors. We ought to check out the freight elevator. That's what we'll have to use, after all."

I shook my head. "We can't check it out right now. You need a letter of permission to use it."

"We could just look it over," Trim said.

Dan started to pace. "Nope, that might be remembered by a bunch of surly security guards. No need to have them mention that Dub here was checking out the freight elevator a few weeks before." He looked at me. "Can't you get one of those letters?"

I blinked. "Actually, I can get one for a hundred bucks."

Trim smiled. "Bribery! I love it! Will you sing to me when we're a few cells apart in the Pen? My God, we're going to be famous!"

I shook my head again, leaned over, and shut off the alarm. The elevator started to move again. "Nope. I can buy one of the surplus desks the company put on sale. We'll have to move it out of here, so we'll get to use the freight elevator prior to the night of the deed. How's that, Dan? We can check it out from the inside."

Dan smiled his broken-nose grin, and I was charmed. "That's good, Dub. We might pull this off yet."

Trim was still grinning. "I think this calls for a liquid lunch, gentlemen!" he said warmly. The elevator touched bottom and he turned to the doors, winking at us. As the doors opened on a group of anxious security people, Trim dashed through them, screaming that we were animals, that he was lucky to be alive. Dan and I stood in the elevator, glanced at each other, then calmly began to walk after him. No one tried to stop us, but they all stared.

"So much for keeping a low profile," I muttered.

"We could always murder him," Dan suggested.

"So much for keeping a low profile!" I grinned.

We had lunch at a bar on eighth avenue, burgers and beers and cigarettes, oh my. We started off talking about the caper, and quickly beered ourselves into discussing our love lives.

"The last time I got laid was two years ago," Trim asserted with a snort. "I've had plenty of opportunities, of course, but the last time I gave in to temptation was two years ago."

"Uh huh," Dan said, starting to get drunk. There was a narrow period during Dan's drinking when he was warm and happy. It quickly descended into melancholy and temper. "And why are you so freakin' noble all of a sudden?"

"I'm keeping my mind sharp," Trim replied. "Nothing fuels artistic ambition like frustration. When I was thirteen I wrote my thirty-seven February Poems while abstaining from masturbation for a month."

Dan looked at me with a wry grin. "You vouch for this poem business?"

I nodded. "I think so. I've seen the poems, and he brags about his self-control so often I think I've been conditioned to believe it no matter what."

"Two years, really?" Dan said.

"Yep."

"And who could have been your downfall, Damien?" I

asked. "I've never known a man who could resist an invitation to love."

Dan giggled at that. Trim took on a pious look.

"Do you really expect me to just announce who my paramours could have been? To shame some poor hussy by admitting she threw herself at me? There are some women with reputations on that list, you know. Could do some damage." He knocked back the last of his beer. "Besides, I don't want to sink to the level of you jackals."

I snorted. "When you speak of plenty of 'opportunities', do you include unconscious women at parties?"

He blinked. "Well, yes, of course."

Dan roared with laughter. Then we all did. The waitress came over to investigate, and we ordered more beers. I spared myself a surreptitious look at my watch and decided I could go another twenty minutes or so without getting fired.

"And you, Dub?" Trim asked wolfishly. "How's your love life these days?"

"Terminal," I lied, thinking of Christine. "No one will touch me."

I wasn't sure why I wanted to keep that to myself. I just did.

"Must be the venereal disease I told everyone you suffer from," Trim said sagely. "According to my latest lies, the madness and brain rot should set in soon."

"Ho, ho," I said in mock anger. "Let's change the subject. Dan, you have any lusty stories to tell us? True ones, at any rate?"

"Or lies," Trim put in immediately. "I don't care."

Dan smiled smugly. "Well, you know, ever since Meredith tap-danced on my heart and left me—"

"I prefer *dumped*," Trim pointed out.

"—I haven't been too interested," he finished.

"Yeah," I said heavily, trying to convey sympathy. I was searching for something encouraging to say when he looked at us with a gleam in his eye.

"But, there has been one interesting evening in my recent days."

Trim and I looked at each other with raised eyebrows. "You old dog," Trim guffawed. "You're holding out on us!"

"I'm supposed to keep you updated on my sex life?" Dan asked.

"Damned right," I agreed earnestly. "It's all we have, really."

Dan grinned. "Well," he said slowly, obviously savoring the moment, "there's a certain waitress we know—"

"Chick?!" Trim burst out. "Don't *tell* me you shagged Chick Parker."

Dan grew somber. "I shagged Chick Parker." Then he grinned again.

My throat had gone dry. "What happened?" I managed.

Dan shrugged. "I'd been in Rue's two weeks ago, getting really drunk. I was by myself, feeling low, and Chick was on, but there was no one else in the place. She kept me company and stayed after her shift to drink with me. We talked a lot, about Meredith, about other stuff, and by two o'clock we were both really drunk, and getting kind of flirty. One thing led to another, and . . . "

I lost track of the conversation then. Trim pumped Dan for details: positions, quantity, quality, atmosphere, etc. I barely heard. Something had come loose, and I had to batten down the hatches before I did something weird. By

the time I managed to swim back to the surface, Trim was
looking at me.

"You okay, Dub?"

"Yeah," I said calmly. "Gotta get back to work, though."

Dan was still reliving the moment. "It was . . . nice, you
know? Just very sweet. We're still friends."

I made my legs work, in desperation.

Back at work, I dragged myself into the lobby and tried not
to catch Dame's eye. It was hopeless. The woman sat in
one place for seven hours a day. If she didn't jump on
every new thing that came her way, and jump hard, no
doubt she would lose her mind.

As if that meant anything when you're stapled to a
cushion all day, bleating into phones and breathing the
fumes of strangers.

"Such interesting friends!" she bleated at me.

"Yes, they are," I bleated back, smiling as best I could.

"Have you known them long?"

I wondered what had kindled this level of interest, if
maybe this was a manifestation of that elderly affliction—
Desperation Talk—the point old people reached where
they would talk to anyone, about anything, just to have
human contact. I wondered if it manifested itself earlier in
receptionists. I kept my grin in place and nodded enthusiastically.

"Years."

"That's sweet."

It wasn't sweet. Trim was a cocksucking arrogant smart-
ass who couldn't spare a kind word, and Dan was an
empty lush who had nothing to say and who had shagged

Chick Parker. I hated them both, and wanted to tell Dame that. Wanted to yell it at her.

Instead I remembered that she was our stooge, and I just smiled.

9. Distractions

SHE KEPT ME IN A BOX SOMEWHERE, took me out when she wanted to look me over and maybe ooh and aah over me a bit, then wrapped me up in tissue paper and put me back, carefully. I wasn't sure what I was to Chick Parker, but it certainly wasn't what she was to me. And the day after our scouting trip at work I woke up in the morning with the most remarkable sense of not giving a shit—I was almost cheerful about it all.

In the shower, I contemplated my sudden burst of good cheer and wondered if it was just a hysterical reaction to the simple fact that Chick Parker apparently found every other man alive on this earth more sexually exciting than me. To prove that this wasn't the case, I called her immediately out of the shower.

"Hello?"

"Hey."

"Dub? It's eight in the morning."

"I know. What are you doing tonight?"

"Uh (yawn) nothing, I don't think. Why?"

"Let's get a drink after your shift."

"Um, okay. I get off at ten."

"I'll be there."

"Okay. Hey, Dub?"

"Yeah?"

"Is everything okay? You sound a little weird."

"Everything," I said cheerfully, "is fine."

"Good. See you later, then?"

"See you later."

I stared at the phone and listened to the dial tone for a moment before hanging it up. Then I stared at it again for a while. Then I got dressed and went to work, because, as usual, I had nothing better to do. At work I sat at my desk all day waiting for the phone to ring. For the first time in the two years I'd worked there, it didn't. With the dumb insistence of the inanimate, my phone sat there, quiet, not ringing, the little red light for voicemail not lighting up, nothing. I grew to hate my phone by the end of day. Not because I expected anyone in particular to call, but because no one called. I was adrift.

At five o'clock I found myself without a single reason to stay, or a single piece of work done. The work didn't bother me, really, but the zombie-like fashion I'd approached the day with bothered me, in a numb way I didn't know how to get around. I could feel myself going blank, filling up with cotton, white nothing. I sat at my desk for a few minutes, staring at a blank computer screen and thinking a flat line, until my eyes caught sight of the time, and I threw my coat on and left. I didn't know what I was waiting for. I didn't have anything to think about, anyway.

I walked around for a little bit, feeling my beard scratching against my shirt, which had been white when I'd bought it a few months ago but was quickly graying to the color of most of my other clothes—just like me, just like everything I had: grayed. Faded. I pushed through all the idiots in their blue suits and tan raincoats, all the women teetering around in their tiny high heels, grimly determined to walk on their tiptoes all the way up the corporate ladder, all the tourists, staring at me goggle-eyed as I made my obscurely hungover way down fifth avenue.

When I made my way up to my apartment, sifting through an endless pile of junk mail and bills, I paused between the third and fourth floors to stand there and wonder when the last time I'd gotten a regular letter had been. I think I'd been eight. I still had two hours before I met Chick, and I had no idea what to do with myself.

I fixed a gin and tonic just to keep myself busy, went out on the fire escape with the phone, and sat there, shivering in the freezing November evening. I watched my neighbors stare back at me, for a few moments, and then the phone rang. It was Trim.

"Hey, I'm at the store."

"Hey."

This seemed to satisfy him. "Where are we meeting later?"

I blinked. "What?"

"Chick called me," he replied. "Said we were getting a drink with her after her shift. Where, if not the Morgue?"

I was shaking my head. "Call Chick," I heard myself say really slowly. "I could give a fuck where."

"My, aren't we surly today," he said amiably. "Who stepped on your balls today, my little idiot bastard?"

Little idiot bastard was a term of endearment for Trim; I knew from bitter experience. "You know something, Trim, you aren't much of a fucking poet."

"It's a tragedy," he admitted easily. "I guess we're just meeting Chick at Rue's?"

My life had shrunk to this point, by small increments over the years. I remembered in high school I was going to write the Great American Novel and see the world. Now my big concern was where to meet Chick and Trim for drinks, as if we didn't do this every night, every week.

I laughed a little at myself. "Yeah, Damien," I said quietly, "just meet us at Rue's and we'll decide from there. Sorry, I think our little scheme has me on edge."

"Well then," he answered cheerfully, "a few drinks will stand you well. Don't sweat it: everything's set. When are we getting the truck?"

"Frankie tells me right before the party," I answered promptly. "I hope you can drive a stick."

"Nope." It sounded like he was eating something.

I blinked. "Do you think Dan can?"

"Nope."

I didn't know what to say. After a few seconds Trim cleared his throat.

"I don't suppose you can?"

"Nope."

There was a moment, and then we both started to laugh. Within a few moments, I was leaning over the railing of my fire escape, whooping into the chill air, getting some minor stares, and feeling a lot of my bad mood evaporate.

"Oh, man," Trim gasped in my ear, "we really are idiots, aren't we?"

"Fuck yeah," I sighed, grinning. "See you later, Capone."

I hung up on Trim, laughing.

And so I sailed into Rue's Morgue an hour and a half later in good spirits, still chuckling a little. The place was strangely crowded, filled with steam and the murmuring pigeon-buzz of a drunken crowd.

I had a moment, when I walked in: the knot of people warming drinks by the door were all people I knew and who knew me, and when I pushed in out of the cold with my hair in a gumby-electric shock standing up and my old, worn, ugly-as-sin sports jacket hanging nattily from my shoulders, they all let out a yell.

"Dub!" they shouted.

I smiled back through a haze of shocked pleasure. A guy named Jim Conklin clapped me on the shoulder. "It's one of those full-moon nights," he said gregariously. "The gang's all here."

It is certainly a thrill to walk into a bar and have everyone shout your name.

I got involved in three conversations at once and was saved by Chick scrambling over and laughingly grabbing my hand, yanking me in mid-sentence away from the door-crowd and over to where she and Trim and Dan were sitting at the bar. Dan and Trim were singing "Mexican Radio," badly, and they weren't even *that* drunk.

"It's a goddamn party," I observed brilliantly.

Chick giggled. "The mojo certainly has risen, Dub," she bubbled. "And it's all your fault."

I grinned. "How?"

"After you called me, you put me in the mood for a drink, and then Conklin called, and then I called a few people, and before too long I was throwing a fucking party right here at work!" she said happily. "And if you had never called me this morning, it wouldn't have happened."

I accepted a beer from Trim, who was still singing with Dan. We nodded at each other and he shook his head at me, and for the first time in a while I remembered why I liked Trim so much. It didn't last too long, but it was a nice reminder.

I tried not to look at Chick and Dan; I was in a good

mood so the idea of the two of them wasn't haunting me the way it had for the past few days, but I also didn't want to think about it, so I didn't. Instead, I thought about the ancient and remarkable Volkswagen Rabbit that Chick drove. I leaned to her ear, trying not to think evil things.

"Hey," I said, "you drive a stick, don't you?"

"Yeah." She blinked against my cheek. "Why?"

I winked. "I need a lesson."

"Really?" she pulled away. "Sure, that would be fun! Why?"

I shrugged. "Survival. If the bomb drops, I might need to know. Can't be choosy in those situations, after all."

"Okay. We'll set up a time."

I nodded. "Soon."

She looked at me. "Why do you have to know, all of a sudden?"

I shrugged again. "I might be getting my Uncle's old car," I lied, pretty baldfacedly. "I want to be able to drive it the minute I get it."

She squinted at me. "All right, when?"

I punched up my mental calendar, which was never very accurate. I never knew what day it was, or how many days were in each month. "How about this Saturday?"

She nodded. "It's a date."

I had a visceral urge to ask her about Dan. *Speaking of dates,* I would say, and ask her with faked nonchalance. We were having a vacuum moment, just looking at each other with nothing to say, while Trim and Dan sang "Mexican Radio" in their warbling, drunken way, and I could have asked. I had to know. I wanted to torture myself. I realized with a start that torture was what my whole attitude was about.

Instead I pulled out a pack of cigarettes and glanced over at Trim and Dan. Putting an arm around her and feeling her mold herself against me in a friendly fashion, for once in my life I didn't let my small side get the better of me.

"For God's sake!" I yelled at them. "In the name of decency! I implore you!"

Trim took that as a request for some solo scat singing. Booze can make the squarest people hipsters for a night, and Trim was halfway to the rat pack as it was. I grinned at what passed for my best male friends these lean days and leaned in, gathering the two of them into my arms and rudely excluding Chick.

"If either one of you mention the caper tonight in my presence," I said jovially, "there will be hell to pay. Get it?"

Trim just sang louder, but Dan clapped me on the back. "I could use a break, too, now that you mention it."

I nodded and pulled away, but it wasn't really the break I was looking for. It felt like the first normal evening to happen to me in a long time, and I wanted it to last. Tomorrow we could plan and plot, tonight I just wanted to be twenty-five again.

"Whew!" Chick snorted as we surfaced. "Testosterone!"

"Bugger," Trim said, and then winked. "It's the nicest word I can think of, unfortunately. I think you know your other choices."

She smiled at him diplomatically, then steered me away. "You and me," she said cheerfully, "have got to talk—"

My heart jumped.

"—about Christine."

"Christine?" I got nervous. "You know Christine?"

She slapped me lightly on the shoulder. "You idiot, I introduced you to Margaret, remember? Of course I know

Christine." She smiled primly. "And I know something you don't: she likes you. A lot. And she wants to know why you haven't called her."

I lost my smile. "I'd rather shoot myself in the head, Chick."

She blinked at me. "Wow. She seemed to think you liked her. I wonder why."

I reddened and steered her toward a vacant inch of floor. "Not fair. No, she was very cool, actually, in her own way."

She shrugged. "Well, you banged her. If you thought she was okay, then what?"

I tried to convey defeat with a shrug. "It's just so . . . small."

"Small?"

"I mean, is this what it comes down to? This mad scramble for a significant other? It's sort of desperate. We go out once, she jumps me like a sailor on shore leave, and we're supposed to be measuring each other for a fucking wedding? Uck, it drives me crazy. It's just desperate."

She rolled her eyes at me. "Jesus, Dub, you're such a fucking *guy* sometimes. What's wrong with just liking someone and wanting to see them again? Why can't it be that simple?" She pushed a finger into my chest. "You're just scared, so you hide behind this vague elitist argument."

She was right, of course, but lord help me I wasn't going to just admit it, so I warmed up to the argument, even as the ironic undertones scratched at the edges of my good cheer. "Because it isn't that simple, Chick, it isn't. Are you going to tell me that if I called her and went out again, that she wouldn't take that as some sort of holy goddamn sign that I was interested?"

"Well, of course."

I smiled at her. "And ask me if I believe that every woman in the world doesn't take that six hundred miles farther and decide we're an item?"

"Nope. The fact that you slept with her she might, but not that."

I gave her my sly squint. "Come on, Chick," I complained.

"We're not all mayun-hungry predators, Dub."

"Ah," I replied, "but Christine *is*."

"Why *are* you doing this, Dub?"

Trim was leaning on Dan's head, which had conveniently hit the table an hour before. He was smoking a cigarette, and we were having a quiet talk at the bar while Chick said good night to some of the diehards.

"The caper?"

He nodded at me drunkenly. "The caper."

I reached over and plucked the cigarette out of his hand. "Trim," I said slowly, feeling eloquent, "this job I have, it isn't what I'm meant to do. And I'm afraid that the time is approaching when it might become the only thing I *can* do."

He stared at me for a moment.

I sighed. "I need to break out of this rut, Trim. I need to do it now, or I'm going to be pushing paper for the rest of my life."

He grinned at me. "I thought this was all about money for you?"

"Oh, it is," I replied. "It's the same thing, don't you see?"

"With that amount of money," I said clearly, "I can pay my debts and buy a car. Think about it. Debt-free and mobile."

Trim smiled. "Dub, you get more human the more dishonest you become. I love that about you, you know that?"

"Everything's about money," I said with a shrug, "even my salvation."

"Salvation?" He began to stroke Dan's hair; Trim didn't miss a chance to be weird. "I like that. It's got that blaze-of-glory feel to it. It's only three weeks away, you know."

"Oh, I know," I said. "Everyone in the office is drooling over the open bar and free disco."

"What are these travesties like?"

I winked. "Oh, they're jolly affairs, all right. They ply us with second-shelf liquor, rubber chicken, and a DJ hired straight out of the prom from hell, make a few speeches about how wonderful we are as human beings, and then they tell us to take our fifty-dollar bonus and get the hell out of dodge. Everyone gets drunk, there's usually a few furtive and slightly desperate flirtations, all with the seamy scent of loss and confusion about them, at least one major faux pas, which results in severe character suicide, and one crying jag on the part of the editorial assistants." I grinned at him. "It's peachy."

Trim seemed to be studying Dan's neck, bare and pale. "I read somewhere that every year two thousand people lose their jobs as a direct result of their actions at the holiday party."

"I believe it," I said earnestly.

"Don't," he said, suddenly looking at me heavily, "let it happen to you."

We cackled, and Chick came over to join us. I was amazed at the lack of rancor I felt toward her. I wondered if I was maturing, and immediately rejected the idea.

"What are my two writer friends talking about?"

"Crime and salvation, sex and longing," Trim said promptly.

"Hey, Adrian," I said good-naturedly, "can I tell you a secret about your writer-friends?"

She offered me a shy smile. "Why, certainly, sir."

I leaned in. Comically, Trim also leaned in, pushing his ear out at us. "We're not very good writers."

Trim hooted with laughter, and Chick giggled. We were all just pleasantly drunk, and we had closed the bar. And Dan. I wondered when I was going to decide whether I liked or hated my friends.

10. Angel-Headed Hipsters

Dub

alarm went off and I surged up from the pillows into the frigid air of my room, desperate to silence its wail, slapping madly until I hit the sweet snooze button, nine minutes of peace and quiet and I slumped back to the warmth of my blankets. It was seven in the morning and I'd been dreaming of something, something, me and Margaret

alarm went off and I surged up from the pillows into the frigid air of my room and hit the snooze button with deceptive skill, my body dredging up memories of being in shape and taken care I didn't realize it still had access to. I sat, slumped, staring at 7:09 AM. I fell backward into the pillows again, stretching luxuriously and cracking my back, shutting my eyes and wondering what I'd been dreaming of . . . horses? cats? something

alarm went off and I surged up from the pillows into the frigid air of my room and hit the snooze button all wrong, knocked the clock off my night table and onto the floor, where it continued to wail at me, too loud, everyone must hear it, it must be waking up the whole fucking block at

7:18 AM with the silken sounds of Deep Purple, Christ of all the stations I had to choose from, why this? I sat in the evaporating warmth of my blankets for a moment, studying the sunlight as it wormed its way into my room from behind the shades, feeling it all seep back into me: it was Thursday, I had to go to work, I had to shower, shave, find clean clothes, tie my tie, make lunch, scrounge for change for the bus, turn the fucking alarm off . . . .

Silence. I was beginning to shiver, the bare floor of my bedroom was freezing, the dimmed air frigid, my walls veined with ice. Still, I squatted by my defeated clock and rubbed my eyes for a moment, did some calculations, which led me to believe I'd done this same morning ritual almost seven hundred times.

I walked to the bathroom, scratching my beard, and turned the hot water up all the way in the shower. I stared at myself until the mirror steamed up, and then got naked and dove in, adding cold water to the mix for my own sanity, lathering up and just standing there. The cocksuckers who shared my water supply began to assert themselves: my water went cold, then hot, then settled into lukewarm. I struggled stupidly to bring back the scalding heat, gritting my teeth against pounding the walls and screaming like Tarzan, a rebel yell that would bring all the local wildlife (pigeons, rabid dogs, feral cats, squirrels, rats, and roaches) to my aid.

Then I rinsed off and turned off the water. I stood there dripping, pushing my hair out of my eyes. I hoped I was burning the skin off of someone.

I shivered back to my room and dressed: thermals, tan khakis, blue workshirt, black socks. Brushed my hair back.

Put on my jellybean tie, my black Chucks, tucked a pair of sunglasses in one pocket. I checked my change bowl and grabbed a handful. I picked out a book to read on the bus and grabbed my backpack to shove it into. Back to the kitchen, where I made a sandwich, scooped up my wallet and keys, pulled on a jacket left there conveniently the night before, and left without a glance back.

It was 8:23 AM. It almost always was.

The bus was seething with violence and cuss words. The man sitting next to me with the vague smell and the slicked-back hair was muttering profanities to himself, and I was pretending not to hear him, filling up with frustration and cowardice. I was reading *To Kill a Mockingbird* again, a dog-eared copy I'd had for fifteen years. I squinted at it and concentrated, trying to forget all the people around me who seemed poised at any moment to take control of the bus, because they apparently believed they knew how to drive it better.

We stalled in traffic again and mutiny threatened. I sank down into my seat and tried to think about anything but the assholes robbing me of my morning. I thought about the sixty-three dollars I had to my name until payday. I thought about Chick and the sad way she seemed completely unattracted to me. I thought about getting no mail again yesterday, about having no messages on my machine, about all the little mementos I had from the times when I used to acquire mementos, all of them dusty with age. I thought about my mom, and how I hadn't thought about her in days.

Thinking wasn't working, so I went back to grim reading until we were at my stop.

Then I was walking. Sifting through all the cocksuckers who worked in the city with me, the blue suits and tan coats, all of them seemed to know some fundamental rule of life I was missing out on. Then I was at work. I stood outside for a moment, unwilling to go in.

I bought a cup of bitter coffee at the newstand in the lobby and crawled to the elevators, nodding to whomever I recognized. I took the elevator up and steeled myself for Dame's cheery good morning. Then I was at my desk, the little light on my phone blinking, e-mails on my computer, rock and roll on my radio, kicking my sneakers off and slipping my cracked and aged shoes on. Then I sat there for a minute, catching my breath, which is what I did for the rest of the day.

TRIM

Trim woke up at eight o'clock and, knowing full well he had to open the video store by eight-thirty, rolled over and went back to sleep. He noted his pounding head and sore throat with clinical expertise, knowing hangovers better than almost any other subject.

At eight twenty-five, using some internal discipline the naked eye could not observe much less suspect existed, he sat bolt upright in bed and opened his eyes. He was still fully dressed, except for shoes.

For a moment, he sat there and moaned.

Then he levered himself to the floor, pulled on his jacket, and picked up his backpack, the contents of which never altered. He slung it over one shoulder and left the apartment, a look of grim determination on his face. Outside, in the cold air, he paused to light a cigarette, then walked three blocks to the store. He got there at eight thirty-five, and, as usual, there was no one waiting to get in.

Opening the store, for Trim, consisted of only three steps: unlocking the doors, turning on the lights, and opening the register. In the employee handbook there were many other such steps, but Trim had taken the time to actually black most of them out, leaving only three sentences behind. Whenever anyone noticed the black marker, he was at a loss to explain why he'd felt it necessary to document his bad work ethic.

He sat down behind the counter, put his feet up, closed his eyes, and entered into a semi-trance he'd perfected back in school. Ostensibly asleep, the slightest noise or change in air pressure roused him to an almost instant state of alertness.

His first customer didn't arrive until ten o'clock. The old man dropped off some adult videos and shuffled away without saying a word. Trim didn't move except to pop open one eye, and then close it again.

At ten-thirty, the phone rang, and this time Trim kept his eyes closed as he snaked out one arm to answer it.

"Moto Video, this is Damien."

He listened impassively. "Hey, Harry."

Again he listened. "No problem. Jimmy's coming in at three, right?"

He nodded. "Okay then. Yeah. Bye."

Smoothly, he replaced the phone, and was still again until eleven, when he roused himself to order lunch and look the place over. Some of the homebodies were trickling in by then, looking for ways to waste time. Some of them, he knew, came in every day, frittering away endless hours in front of bad movies that hadn't even been released to the big screen. He regarded them with a blank, slightly dim look and a monosyllabic vocabulary that discouraged small talk except in the loneliest and leechiest of them, whom he felt compelled to ignore completely.

As the afternoon wore on, he became more and more animated, until he was walking the aisles and hopping over the counter. When Jimmy arrived at three, Trim jumped up and called out his name with enthusiastic gusto, grinning from ear to ear and chatting amiably as he picked up his jacket, bag, and free videos, walking out the door not even a minute after Jimmy had shown up. He paused just outside to light a new cigarette, and walked home to begin his day.

Dan

There was nothing on TV. As usual. There was nothing in the fridge except ice and baking soda. There was no noise in the place, just the muffled darkness of five in the morning. There were no more cigarettes in the pack on the coffee table, no more magazines unread in the bathroom, no more butane in the lighter, and no more reasons to stay awake.

He flipped the channels anyway: infomercials, deadhead talk shows, commercials, test patterns, old movies, snow. He and Trim had no money for cable so there were thirteen channels to blow through. He did it twice more just in case, then shut the TV off. The click was deafening, the silence following more so. He sat in the easy chair and stared at the fading glow on the screen for a few moments, breathing heavily and imagining he could see the alcohol leaving his body with every exhalation. He hadn't been very drunk that day: he couldn't afford to be drunk anymore, unless someone was around to buy the drinks.

He glanced at his watch. He knew that Trim set his alarm for eight o'clock every fucking goddamn morning and he made it his business to not be there when the bastard woke up. He hated mornings, and preferred to face them alone, and the worst part of having a roommate, he'd always thought, was having to see him in the morning, fighting for the bathroom, drinking coffee, making small talk.

He considered his options, tracing his fingers over the remote control in the brightening dark.

He pulled himself up from the chair, twisting himself around until his back cracked. Slowly, he pulled together the remnants of his life: wallet, keys, jacket, shoes. Spare change. Matches. Equipped, he made his way carefully from the apartment, not wanting to wake up his roommate. In the cold air, he allowed himself to make a little more noise as he walked. There was an all-night diner a few blocks away that didn't seem to mind him when he nursed coffee there for a few hours in the mornings. He bought an early-edition paper on the way and even got a smile from the tired and familiar hostess when he walked into the diner. He ordered coffee and opened the paper, beginning on page one and reading carefully, slowly, taking in every story.

DJB

At four thirty, Wendy from customer service sent me an e-mail suggesting we all go out for a bitchfest-cum-after-work cocktail, because she'd had a rough day and needed to decompress. I replied that I'd be glad to join her, but that I couldn't stay late. I liked Wendy. Eight months before, I'd asked her out and she'd gently told me no way, and since then we'd managed to remain friendly, and every now and then we had lunch or went out for a drink. I no longer wanted to date her, though I occasionally day-dreamed of sleeping with her.

By five after five, we had gained three more socializers, which wasn't so bad. Wendy was a good-looking Jewish girl who often found herself with more friends than she knew what to do with, most of them male, and I was used to sharing her with other people; I wasn't the sort of guy that inspired girls who had racks like Wendy's to pay attention exclusively to me. I wasn't sure what kind of guy I was, but it wasn't that type, for sure.

We went to an uptight Manhattan bar, mostly white with a few exceptions, and ordered mixed drinks to show we weren't proles. I could tell it was going to be the sort of night I really couldn't afford: raucous, later than intended, and with a drink bill the size of the Milky Way. I started off with a scotch on the rocks to prove my manhood, kept trying to keep Wendy for myself despite the obvious futility of the endeavor, and the evening was pretty much down-hill from there. The hell of your cubicle friends in the city, I knew, was the amount of time you spent having drinks and talking to people you really didn't like very much. I ended up with Mario.

Mario was in my department but under a different boss, and I had a nodding relationship with him on most days: nodded hello to each other and left it at that.

This time, however, we found ourselves sitting next to each other in a bar with a few drinks behind us, and it seemed to Mario that it would be good to ask me a few probing questions about myself, since Wendy with the oh-so-delicate features and nice rack was paying more atten-tion to Mike from finance than to either one of us. I quickly grew to resent this tactic of Mario's, and attacked him with thinly veiled sarcasm.

The joke was on me, though: the guy whose name I can't remember leaves early, and Wendy and Mike leave a few minutes later in a suspicious coupling. Mario and I are left sitting alone in a booth, sipping drinks.

"You ever wonder why you bother, Phil?" he asked in a desultory monotone. I guess he was drunk.

"All the time," I replied.

"Can I tell you something?" he asked.

I tensed up, but what could I say? Besides "Sure."

"I like her," he said slowly. "Wendy, I mean."

I nodded. "Oh yeah?"

"I think I love her."

This struck me as funny, and I let a short laugh escape. This made Mario angry. He stood up.

"Fuck you, man," he said angrily, and left.

I can't explain what I think was so funny about this. My own issues of unrequited love? The fact that Mario had suddenly decided that a few months of hellos in the hallway meant we were close enough friends for that conversation? Or the fact that he'd stiffed me on the bill? It didn't matter. I left laughing.

I couldn't wait for Christmas.

TRIM

After sleeping most of the afternoon and early evening, Trim woke up to shower and make a few calls. The calls were usually to the same people and usually resulted in the same actions. He splashed on some aftershave, pushed his hair out of his face by way of combing it, and put on his usual outfit: worn jeans, white oxford, black sports jacket. He wore the same clothes more often than not, and had since the age of sixteen, when he'd heard that Albert Einstein had done so to conserve his precious mental energies. He pulled on a pair of combat boots he'd had since the age of fourteen, stuffed his wallet and keys into his back pockets, made sure there were cigarettes (most likely stale) in the jacket, and went out to meet his cronies for drinks.

They met at Rue's Morgue, usually, and sat in the rear even on rainy Tuesdays when all the sane souls stayed home to drink. Trim chaired the meetings, which meant he watched everyone intently, doled out healthy doses of sarcasm and insult, and forced everyone to listen to his poetry by sheer force of personality.

As the night wore on and they got drunker, the sarcasm got sloppy, the laughter louder, the poetry much, much worse.

At a quarter after nine, Trim stood on his chair, raised his glass to the ceiling, and said:

"The city regards me with blank, dulled eyes / clouded store windows smog covered lights / it serves me watery drinks in smoky dive bars / which are what it passes as delights."

They broke into wild applause, causing the bartender to glance up and wonder briefly if he should throw them out early this night.

"My God," said Karyn with the bad teeth, "I can't believe it. That one's the worst yet!"

And they broke into laughter as Trim sat down, grumbling. "You idiot bastards wouldn't know good free verse if it crawled up your asses to die peacefully where no one would ever look for it."

She snorted. "I've got more free verse up my ass than you've ever understood, my little Iago."

Trim snorted back. "Fuck you. More beer?"

DAN

Aprici's never had more than twelve customers, and Dan suspected that they normally didn't add anyone until one of the veterans died, preferably of some liver-related ailment. Perhaps they had made an exception for him, a sort of grandchild clause.

He liked Aprici's because it opened at seven in the morning.

Dan thought he was starting to look a lot like the usuals at Aprici's. He had read once, back when he could amuse himself by reading, that people had a tendency to resemble their spouses and pets, over time. He supposed it was due to the amount of time they spent with each other, and if that were true he was in serious trouble, considering the mugs of his fellow patrons. The thought made him smile briefly as he made his way through a beer and the sports page.

Through the murky plate window, he watched normal people walking to work, to the bus, buying papers and coffee, and pushing rudely past each other. He studied them for a long time.

"Hey, kid," the bartender taunted, "you see a ghost?"

Dan supposed he would be known as "kid" until he was seventy in a place like Aprici's. He let his gaze linger on the outside world for a few seconds more.

"Yeah."

11. The Day Before

DAN WAS DRIVING US IN HIS CAR, an ancient Chevy Malibu with a hole in the floor you could see the road through, a knock in the engine that made me nervous, and theoretical brakes. The radio only picked up AM, and the inspection sticker on the windshield was so old it had faded to a sort of gray smudge. He hadn't driven it in a few weeks, not having the money for gas anymore or anyplace, really, to go, so it was smoking like a three-alarm fire as we coughed down a minor highway in Jersey. The heat didn't work either, and I huddled with Trim in the back seat, wondering if we'd frozen together, spot-welded.

Trim was reading my mind. "I think we're turning Siamese, *mia fraccacio.*"

"Kiss me, you fool," I said dryly. This made us laugh.

"Now, wouldn't that be embarrassing if saliva fused us together in that pose, huh?" he cackled, his breath a cloud that obscured him for a moment.

"Shut up," Dan growled. He was hungover. "I'm trying to drive."

"You know," Trim replied brightly, "seeing double doesn't mean you can drive twice as well."

"Fuck you both. I'm looking for a sign; we should have hit route 130 already."

"How the hell would you know?" I asked. "You've been to Jersey, what, three times in your life?"

"Shut up."

It was the day before my office party, and we were meeting Frankie to pick up the van in some backwater Jersey hamlet. I had twenty-five hundred dollars in an envelope in my pocket, scraped together from my meager savings, Trim's nonexistent savings, Dan's most recent unemployment check, and my credit cards. We looked at it as an investment, but the price was leaving us all a bit grumpy. Well, Dan, anyway.

I wasn't sure when the idea of the caper became an everyday bit of knowledge, when exactly we stopped oohing and aahing over it as if it were amazing to us that we were undertaking something so blithely illegal and probably doomed. We sat in Dan's deathmobile and waited to pick up a stolen vehicle so we could rob my place of employment as if it were something we'd done before, taken a class in as kids, or something. I looked out the window, and the rest of the world went by without comment, wet and cold and smoky, and the two men I'd pinned my hopes to with sinking heart and weak-kneed faith had become my world, lonely and distant.

Trim was unshaven and wild-haired, wearing his big tweed longcoat and military boots (which he called his Stomping Boots, telling anyone who'd listen that he intended someday to become a skinhead and stomp those of lesser genetic material) and his sunglasses, just to be rude. He was nervous, though. It robbed him of some cheer, and I must admit I'd never seen the bastard afraid. I could feel it seeping off him like oil off water, pooling next to me and staining the cracked vinyl of the seats. In the face of it, he was trying to be cool, cracking jokes, but I could feel him quivering there, and for a change I looked to Dan for support. Dan remained a saint, although his tarnish was eating away at him. He still had his principles, even if they weren't worth shit.

A song came on the crappy AM station, which had been fading in and out of the speakers for the past ten minutes. Trim sat up straight.

"I know that," he pronounced with a grin my way. "That's 'Badfinger'."

Trim knowing anything about Badfinger momentarily fascinated me. "I thought you only listened to bands like 'Nitzer Ebb' and 'Death'."

He looked down at me haughtily. "I'll have you know that all we serious death-rock-loving poets have strong roots in candy pop."

"Lies!" I accused.

"Fucking shut up!" Dan hissed. "I can't drive with you chimps swinging around back there!"

"Oooh eeeh aaaah aaaaaah!" Trim let loose, scratching his armpits.

We fell into a grumpy silence then.

I always liked driving at night. I liked to just stare out the window and feel the hum of the car, space out a little and wonder about all the places we were passing, what it was like there, what the people did, if there were any good stories there. This usually reminded me that I used to like finding good stories, which made me morose, which in turn encouraged me to stare out the window, feeling the hum of the car beneath me . . . which suddenly didn't feel right.

"Everything okay up there?" I asked.

Dan's eyes flicked to me in the rearview. "Uh . . . I think the carb's popped a bolt."

There was a popping noise coming from the engine, growing louder. "What does that mean?"

"Oh, lord . . . " Trim muttered.

"It means we're pulling over," Dan said acidly. "And walking."

"I'm too delicate to walk," Trim announced. "How 'bout I wait here and you pick me up later?"

"Fuck you," Dan said, slamming the car into park on the shoulder. "Get out."

We stood around the car for a moment. Dan had left the headlights on, and the engine ticked and clicked. Trim began shivering comically, and Dan preposterously pulled a bottle of beer from one of his longcoat's pockets.

"She was a good one," he pronounced, "but she goes to a better place." He twisted open the cap and took a slug, his breath steaming out of his nose.

"Uh, Dan, this may not be the best time to stage an intervention—" Trim said slowly, but Dan was shaking his head.

"Fuck off. I ain't driving the van back anyway, right? Let's walk; we're gonna be late as it is. I hope Frankie's a patient cat, Dub."

I didn't want to admit that I didn't know my cousin well enough to say. We started walking along the road, freezing, and I struck up a conversation in self-defense, just to keep us from freezing to death.

"What were you doing this day last year?"

Trim glanced at me. "What?"

"I wonder sometimes how much difference a year makes. It's December twelfth—what were you doing today a year ago?"

"What the fuck you want to know, Dub?" Dan growled.

My teeth were chattering, and I lit a cigarette just to imagine some warmth. "Just thinking, man. Last year on December twelfth I think I was watching TV and eating McDonald's."

Trim cackled, sending great gales of steam into the night. "You can actually remember *watching TV?* Your life must suck, Dub, if TV is big enough to leave an impression."

I put on my best pious expression. "It's just so rare—"

"What," Dan interrupted, "watching TV or actually remembering an evening, you lush?"

"Glass houses," Trim advised, kicking some stones out of his way and snatching my cigarette from between my fingers with practiced ease. "So? You were watching TV. What's so remarkable about that?"

"That twelve months later, I'm about to commit a felony."

"You're not going to get naked, start beating a drum, and tell us how you've never felt so alive, are you?"

I regained my cigarette through physical force. "Maybe."

That got a chuckle out of Trim, but then silence dripped over us and plodded on our words. We moved through the empty waste of Jersey with grim determination and silent resolve, passed by pickup trucks and Trans Ams filled with idiot kids honking their horns at us as if we gave a shit. By the time we saw a sign that said MOORE, 1 MILE we were all concentrating too hard on staying alive in what seemed dangerously frigid conditions to keep up idle chitchat. I began kicking rocks onto the road to amuse myself.

"Stop it, you kneebiter," Trim snapped.

Greasy Tony's advertised the world's largest grease jar, and this didn't raise Frankie up in Trim's opinion. Frankie and Dan seemed to like each other on sight, however, which annoyed me; it made me wonder if I was lacking a certain level of testosterone, maybe, or something. Frankie was sitting at a booth all alone in the rear, and as we steamed into the joint he waved at me.

"About fucking time," he growled, making room for us.

"The car broke down," I said lamely.

"It's still about fucking time."

I swallowed a reply and gestured to Dan. "This is my other partner and friend, Dan Quinn. Dan, my cousin Frankie."

"Frank," he corrected, shaking hands. "Irish, huh?"

Dan actually grinned, lighting a cigarette. "What gave it away? The red nose or the beer in my pocket?"

"Care to share?" Frank asked.

Dan slipped him a beer under the table. The two of them kicked back in a relaxed manner and sipped their beers and smoked. I glanced at Trim, and the bastard just shrugged.

"You got my cut?" Frankie asked with a belch.

I pulled out the envelope, weighed it in my hand for a moment with a sudden reluctance to go through with this, and slid it over to my cousin. He did me the honor of not counting it, but just pocketed it and gave me a wink.

"All right, cuz," he said cheerfully. "I have to admit I'm impressed." He winked at Dan, and I wanted to throttle the both of them. "He should hang out with sports like you more, eh, Quinn?"

Dan just grinned around his cigarette, concentrating on the red coal.

"Well," Frankie said after a moment, "here you go." He slid a set of keys my way. "It's the white EconoVan parked outside, and it's got Jersey plates, which I wouldn't leave on there for more than a day or so. Automatic, so you women won't have any trouble driving it. It's only three years old and runs like a cherry, girls. It don't smoke, all the lights work, and the sticker is current, so I don't see why any cops would want to pull you over. If you see any fucking blue-and-red lights, assholes, hit the gas and pray, 'cause if you get pulled over in this van you're doing time." He winked at me. "And so am I, since I don't doubt for a second how long you'd keep fucking quiet. So run, boys, run if the law reaches out for you, okay?"

I winked at *him*, just to be even. "Just for you, Frankie."

He gave me a look and I tried to match it. Finally, he stood up. "Say hi to your mom, Philly," he said. "Tank's topped off, and I did some work on the engine for you: changed the oil, checked the trans, replaced the shocks. Okay? If it gives you any trouble, you can't blame me." He started to move off.

I found myself obscurely touched by this show of . . . whatever. I touched his arm as he pushed out of the booth, and he bent to look at me.

"Frank," I said suddenly. "Thanks."

He looked around at Trim and then Dan. "Yeah, Phil. Good luck, okay? And say hi to Aunt Gretch."

I nodded. "I will."

Trim waited until he was out the door. "That was very touching. Should we have dinner first, or just get going?"

"Let's eat. I'm starved," Dan said.

I was staring at the keys. "Holy shit," I said quietly. "We're actually going to rob the place."

Trim pounded me on the back. "So we are, boyo."

"Order me some coffee and pie. Cherry pie," I said, standing up. "I'll be right back."

◎

I called Chick Parker at work. I was sweating, and I still had the keys to the van in my hand.

"Dub?" Her voice came on the line, distant and muted. There was a big crowd at Rue's Morgue, apparently.

"Hey, Adrian," I said. "Yeah, it's me. What's up?"

Why we all start our conversations with that inane question, I have no idea.

"Just work; it's really crowded. What's up with you? I don't have much time."

"I'll let you go."

"No, I got a minute or so," she said. "What is it? You sound really weird. As a matter of fact, you've been really weird on and off for a long time now."

I was thrilled that she'd noticed. "Chick, I—I don't know. I got a decision to make."

"About what?"

"About—I can't tell you. But I need help making it."

"But you can't tell me?"

"No." I laughed, because I could picture her face. "Sorry, but I'm not the only one involved, and I don't think I'd tell you anyway if I was."

She took that well. "This isn't going to be easy, Dub. And I've only got a few seconds here, really. The vikings are demanding grog, you know, and my charm over my boss only goes so far."

I bit my lip. "Let me ask you just one question, and your answer will help."

"Okay."

I considered my words. "If you could change your life in one night by doing something you maybe weren't supposed to and which could have grave consequences, would you? Assuming you felt that if you didn't change your life soon you'd end up blowing your brains out?"

"Whoa," she breathed. "I didn't realize this was going to be a big philosophical discussion. You know what, Dub?"

"Yeah?"

"I don't think I've ever known someone like you."

I closed my eyes. I didn't want to hear that. "Chick, focus," I said as cheerfully as possible.

"Right: I say yes. I must put in the disclaimer that I have no details, the possession of which might easily change my answer, but if I felt I needed a change and a chance came up to make it, then yes, even with risks I would go for it."

"Yeah?"

"I said so, didn't I? Look, Dub, I got to go. Are you okay?"

"No, but I will be."

She hesitated. "Promise?"

"Yes."

She hesitated again, and then sighed. "Shit, I gotta go. Listen, call me tonight after three. I'll be home. I want to talk to you more, okay?"

"Okay. Thanks."

Driving home, we discovered that the radio in the van only picked up AM too, and this sent Trim into hysterics.

"I wonder if there's any Nitzer Ebb on AM!" he cackled.

Dan hit the back of his head lightly. "Jesus, be quiet."

"You're fucking antisocial, Daniel," Trim accused, rubbing his head.

"Just toward you," I pointed out.

When we passed Dan's Malibu, we cheered and clapped Dan on the shoulders, which meant we almost ran off the road. I wasn't feeling as anxious as I had been, and managed a few grins even. I began to believe we had it all worked out: everything had worked out so far, and if I could manage to snag Dame's keycard the next day without muffing it, the rest would, I hoped, prove easy.

I remembered Trim telling me that he was the Bill Murray of our little group, that he brought the razzle-dazzle to the party. I reminded him of this, and he laughed. Even Dan smiled.

"I think that makes me Harold Ramis," I offered. "Dan, that unfortunately makes you Dan Aykroyd."

"Dub, you ignorant slut," Dan said quietly as he got comfortable in the back seat, eyes shut. "What are we? Ghostbusters?"

"Nah," Trim disagreed instantly. "In your case, gutbusters."

And that's the way it went all the way home.

I didn't get home until two in the morning, the van quietly put away in a parking garage near work. I turned on a few lights, listened to messages from my mother and from Chick (just stressing that she really wanted to hear from me—I was like a savage on a reservation, ogled and wondered about) and sat down in my big easy chair.

Strangely enough, I planned what I was going to wear the next day.

Casual was the way to go, but on the most important day of my life, I wanted to have some style, too.

Contemplating suspenders, I fell asleep right there in the chair.

12. Beautiful Chaos

I'M NO STRANGER TO FRUSTRATION, and I could sense that the day wasn't going to cooperate from the moment I opened my scabbed-over eyes and saw that it was nine-oh-five in the morning, five minutes after I was supposed to be at work. My back was aching.

I sat up and enjoyed a moment of silence and calm before I struggled on with my day, my plan, my usual crap. The past few weeks were a blur of this and that and a lot of fractured moments, nothing coming together into a coherent whole, and I wanted a few seconds, at least, wherein I was sitting still. Chief Sitting Still, my mind gurgled up, and I managed to laugh at myself.

"Okay," I muttered.

No one cared that I was late, of course; ostensibly we were supposed to work until three o'clock and then head over to the party, but in reality we showed up, took lunch, and then went to the party. I said my hellos, listened to a horrible voicemail from a very upset vice president who called me every name in the book for messing up something or other, then set about stealing keycards.

My plan was simple: I wanted Dame's keycard, but I didn't want to take the chance that she would notice too soon and report it missing, which would mean it would be deleted from the system and I wouldn't be able to use it anymore. So, I first stole one from a guy named Ken West, replacing it with my own. Then I switched Ken's with Cassie's, Cassie's with Misty's, Misty's with Jeof Vita's, Jeof's with Danette's and finally Jeof's with Dame's. I distracted them all with champagne, and the switching was actually easier than I would have thought. I wondered if maybe I had more of Frankie's genes than I might have guessed.

This way, if anyone noticed anything—which was doubtful—Dame's wouldn't be switched off. I stole my own keycard back from Ken with some fairly bold daylight desk-rifling, then swaggered back out to have a toast and gaze around at all the loot. My heart was pounding, and everyone was shaking my hand and pounding my back as if they had no idea what kind of man I was.

Confident, I could relax. Within the first half-hour of the company party I had three whiskey sours. They'd seemed weak when I'd tested the first one, but after the third it became obvious that it was all a careful ruse on the part of the bartenders, in order to tempt large tips away from drunken revelers.

I became fascinated by the small dress Wendy was wearing, leering at her owlishly from behind columns, plants, and other people.

Shortly thereafter I reclined with some cronies near one of the bars, listening to dull speeches from the Lords of Our Company; vague, uptight people I didn't know by sight but who, apparently, made a lot more money than me. My cronies, by and large, agreed with my assessment, and we drank to that.

At one point, Wendy pulled me onto the dance floor and I flailed about to "I Will Survive" with a drink in my hand and a plastered expression on my face. Flashbulbs went off, and I knew with a distantly drunk alarm that I was going to regret it all, until the song ended and Wendy crushed me to her, giggling and thanking me for being a good sport. It all seemed worth it.

For a moment.

I smoked two cigarettes with the vice president of marketing, a tall, thin man with bad skin and slicked-back hair who tended to speak in one-syllable words. We were standing near the bathrooms, which is the ancient genetically programmed gathering place for nicotine addicts.

"Like it?" he asked.

"Absolutely," I slurred.

"What do you do here?"

"Editor!"

"Like it?"

"Not even a little bit."

"Shame." He held out his hand. "Tom Ring."

"Marketing," I replied, shaking hands. He made a gun gesture with his other hand, and a clicking noise. I plowed on. "You like it?"

"This?" he asked.

"No, marketing."

"Yep. Have fun."

I felt networked.

Around eight my cronies and I conferred by the plastic plants near the ladies room. We quickly sketched a plan that involved all our cash, a place called Buckman's on

Forty-Ninth, and all the single chicks we could convince to come along. Then we broke the huddle with clapped hands and shouts, and I headed for the pay phones to call Dan, who was waiting by a pay phone for me. Why a pay phone? Trim had told Dan with a straight face that it had something to do with traced calls and CIA gizmos (actually using the term *gizmo*). Later he unnecessarily confided to me that he really just wanted Dan to freeze his balls off. "It'll sober him up," he asserted with the grim humor of someone incapable of fooling even himself, these days.

"Jesus CHRIST what took you so long?" Dan said by way of hello.

"Got bombed," I said honestly.

"Jesus CHRIST that's FUCKING fanTAStic," he bellowed. "MY BALLS are the size of RAISINS."

"We're going to Buckman's," I said genially. I figured my charm had to kick in at some point.

"Where the fuck is THAT?" he shouted. "If you make me walk fifty GODDAMNED blocks in this weather, Dub, I swear—"

"Buckman's," I repeated. "Buck-man's. You've been there."

"No."

I rolled my eyes and told him where it was. "Meet me there. And don't forget Trim."

"I won't forget Trim, you IDIOT," he snapped, and the line went dead in my ear.

I shrugged, studied the phone for a moment, then turned to go hunting for single chicks. The year before, we'd even actually convinced one or two to come along.

It was a Friday night, after all, and Buckman's was packed

with smarmy kids like ourselves, guzzling drinks, smoking ill-advised cigarettes, and trying to get laid, boy and girl alike. It was, in my suddenly boisterous opinion, the closest I ever got to Eden: being twenty-five, drunk as a Carolina hillbilly on payday, surrounded by young women who wanted nothing to do with me, and about to become a criminal.

We took over a table in the back, ordered whiskey all around, and toasted each other's crappy jobs. I was having a great time until Dan and Trim walked in.

I jumped up and thrust out a hand.

"Mi *fraccacios*, como esta por favor! Come warm a glass and I'll introduce you to people you won't like, won't enjoy, and who most probably won't care for you, either!"

There was a round of cheers from behind me.

Dan looked cold enough to piss ice cubes as he stopped to offer me a quick nod and my coworkers a glance over my shoulder and another even quicker nod. Then he turned back to me as Trim sauntered past.

"Christ, I thought we'd have trouble keeping Danny Boy straight," Trim muttered, and then began introducing himself to everyone, including some people who weren't my coworkers. Dan put a hand on my shoulder.

"You okay?"

I smiled my most charming Dublen smile, a gift from my rascal of a father. "C'mon and say hi to everyone."

So we made a big show of carousing. We bought a lot of drinks for various people, made conversation, got loud, and kept an eye on the time. Trim and Dan seemed to stay sober as sand, and I willed myself into their arid atmosphere, with some success.

We made quite an impression and got the whole crowd disgustingly drunk. Trim assigned everyone Indian names: I became One With Runs, which everyone found very amusing; Dan actually unclenched a little and told everyone supposedly hilarious stories about my drinking habits and lack of control, playing up the drunken Irish thing for himself, pounding backs, even hinting at a brogue. I hadn't seen Dan so animated in months, and even though it was a ruse, I liked it. It was nice to know that Dan had someone alive left in him, even if it was just an act.

After about two hours, Trim caught my eye, winked, and announced he was going to the bathroom. Catching my eye again, he actually ran a finger along his nose like the grifters in *The Sting*, the arrogant bastard, and I watched him make his way to the front door and leave, unnoticed, already forgotten. Dan waited a few minutes, and simply stood up laughing and melted outside without a word.

I looked around: no one was paying any attention to me; they were talking to each other, making no sense, being drunk. I stood and turned without a comment and started walking for the doors. I kept waiting for someone to shout out my name, for someone to notice. I fought a mad urge to turn and see if anyone was watching me. A song was playing in my head: *the doc said, what were you thinking 'bout? Bob said, that's just the point, I wasn't thinking about nothing, now I gotta do something else to pass the time.* Over and over again, *the doc said, what were you thinking 'bout? Bob said, that's just the point, I wasn't thinking about nothing.* I started humming it, watching the other beer dicks and office teases with slitted eyes and a careful grin, pulling open the door with a blast of frigid air, and hitting silence as I let the door slide shut behind me. The city seemed still for a moment as I realized things were actually going according to plan.

Trim and Dan were standing on the corner, stamping their feet and sharing a cigarette. Dan waved at me. I stood in front of Buckman's for a second, feeling the city.

"Hey, Dub," Dan yelled, sounding like he was still in a good mood, "while we're young?"

"And poor?" Trim added.

I laughed, and turned to join them.

I had taken the liberty of awarding Gene, the tall and gangly man who would be the lone guard in the lobby of my building in the evening, a bottle of Johnny Walker Red Label. I told him it was because I felt sorry for him being stuck there all night while we partied, and told him some-one had given it to me but I didn't drink scotch—a blatant lie, but Gene wouldn't know that. Gene spoke in carefully minted phrases, and I suspected he had a lot more going for him than a lightweight security job would indicate, which might be why he always got bombed when left alone on the job. Bottom feeding is always depressing.

My plan had worked. When Trim, Dan, and I piled up against the front doors of the building, fumbling for Dame's keycard, Gene was nowhere to be seen. When we burst into the empty lobby with an excited and unwise babble of Trim's bombastic pronouncements ("To glory, boys!") Dan's bitter rebuttals ("How about to jail, bitch, if you don't shut up?") and my own amused commentary ("When are you kids going to stop arguing long enough to realize you love each other?") the coast remained clear.

I suggested quietly that Dan go check the security office to make sure Gene was safely snookered. Trim argued that if we could make it upstairs without being noticed, why risk rousing the guard by snooping around.

"Dub's right," Dan said, shaking his head. "We might make it up, but we got to come down again, right? I'd feel better if I knew the hired walkie-talkie was snoozing in his office."

Trim took on a hurt air. The fucker was nervous as hell, I could see, and that was making me nervous as well. "Fine," he said, "you always take Dub's side."

Dan minced off to the rear of the lobby, looking for Gene, and I found myself standing around with Trim, who was dancing from foot to foot as if he were still freezing.

"Nervous?" I asked.

"At committing a felony at long last?" he said with a raised eyebrow. "You bet your soft white ass I'm nervous."

I chuckled. "Shouldn't take more than an hour or two."

"That's great, Phil," he said without a trace of his usual sarcasm. He hardly sounded like Trim at all. "Don't calm me down, okay? You're no good at it."

We stood in the lobby with our hands in our pockets, waiting. Trim began walking around me in dizzying circles. I had two packets of rubber gloves in my jacket, and I handed him one. He looked them over and then spent a diverting few moments struggling to get them on. I didn't think he'd done it right, but it was close enough.

"Hey, Dub, maybe we should have uniforms."

I blinked at him. His pacing was making me nauseous. "Huh?"

"You know, janitor's uniforms, or something. So we'll look like we belong here."

His eyes had that half-crazy light in them I'd grown used to since college. Here was Trim, older, fatter, somehow darker, and he still dyed his hair blonde, he still wore black just to annoy people, he still worked in a video store because it was easier than almost anything else he could think of. I stared at him for a moment while his ludicrous suggestion hung in the air, and I realized with a sinking feeling, "Jesus, Trim, you think this is a game, don't you?"

He smiled, and I wanted to smack it off him. "Best adventure," he said breezily, "I've had in a while." What I'd taken for genuine nervousness was gone without a trace.

It hit my stomach and I was instantly ill. All this time, all these weeks, and he still didn't take it seriously. It was fun for him. And I hadn't realized. I'd known the fucker for years, and I hadn't realized. He didn't believe that anything could go wrong—it was all just fun. He probably thought, somewhere deep inside, that if everything went wrong we could just apologize and go home.

I sat down on the floor, and Trim grinned down at me. Suddenly, he was joined by Dan. They both stood there, peering at me as if I were undergoing some wonderful transformation.

"You okay, Dub?" Dan asked.

"Sure," I said crisply. "I'm trapped here with a madman, but otherwise I'm fine."

Dan and Trim exchanged a look, as if they were wondering which madman I meant. "Okay, then, I'm going to get the van," Dan said. "Go on up and I'll meet you at the freight elevator."

"Okay," Trim said happily. Then he looked down at me as Dan turned away. "Don't worry, Dub, you're on my time now. My natural luck will carry us both."

"Jesus," I said, standing up on shaky, doomed legs, "I should have drank more."

The office was silent and dark, filled with dust and little else. I wanted to leave the lights off, but Trim snorted and flicked them all on dramatically.

"My kingdom!" he shouted, throwing out his arms.

"Shut up!" I hissed.

He winked, taking me by the arm. "Dub," he said loudly, "if there's no one here we can make all the noise we want. If there are party crashers wouldn't you rather find out now?"

I kept quiet. I didn't like admitting that Trim was right. It went against my sensibilities. We made a quick circuit of the floor, and then checked the time. It was one in the morning, and we were only a few hours away from making the first big score of our lives. I took a deep breath and straightened my tie.

"All right," I said, "let's go find a handtruck."

Trim let out a whoop. "That's the spirit, my friend! Avast ye mateys, back away from yonder treasure or I'll skewer the lot of ya! Aaargh!"

I waited a beat. "That really wasn't the spirit I was trying to convey."

"Duly noted. Handtruck!"

For a bunch of lazy slackers, we found efficiency in crime, moving merchandise like we were getting time and a half for it all, plus benefits. I knew where everything was, and we worked our asses off out of a mixture of desperation, fear, and excitement. Trim raced around the floor, riding the handtruck wildly, me tagging along glumly, feeling sweaty in my khakis and cotton shirt. Usually Trim's insane good cheer infected me and made me looser than I would have been otherwise. This time it made me nervous.

"Do you feel like a criminal?"

I was busily ripping computer cords out of the wall, and sweating up an out-of-shape storm in the process. Trim was smoking a cigarette and sitting on the window sill, and he had somehow gotten over his earlier nervousness enough to have fallen into his philosophy mode.

"I don't know," I panted. "Why?"

"I don't, and it's making me wonder about the nature of guilt and the concept of crime. I don't feel like a crook, and yet we're in the act of grand theft."

"Fascinating," I grumbled. "Are you going to be doing any actual grand thieving, Damien, or are you going to sit on your fat ass all night and contemplate it?" I turned to him with a sudden grin. "Are you gonna do some living, Damien, or are you just going to study it?"

He flicked ashes at me. "Fuck you. Even arch-criminals get breaks, right? I'm union."

I paused. I thought I'd heard something. I held up a hand and, to my surprise, Trim fell silent. We sat there, breathing, for about a half-minute, straining to hear. I began to imagine I could hear the dust thud onto the floor.

Finally I turned to look at Trim. For the first time in my life, I saw him without dark cheer like evil syrup covering his face.

"Let's get a move on, Dub."

I grinned, because for once I could show him how he made the rest of us feel. "You're on."

Dan slammed the door of the van. It was twelve feet of expensive office equipment. Following Tom's advice, we'd left behind peripherals like keyboards, mice, cables, paper cartridges, etc. Still, we all stared at the van for a moment, and Dan shook his head.

"That's forty thousand dollars of office equipment?"

Trim put his arm around him. "Let's not count the beans right here on the street, okay? We could fit our entire apartment in that van, and some of those computers retail for five, six grand each. Stop kvetching and drive."

"You know where you're going?" I asked. Uncle Tommy had stipulated that Dan drop the van alone.

"For Christ's sake, Dub," Dan growled.

I scrutinized him. "You idiot. You've been cadging beers down here."

He clenched his teeth. "Back down, Dub."

"What, are you some fucking alcoholic, Dan?" I shouted. "Or maybe you're just an asshole? I swear to fucking God, Dan, if you get DUI'd in this fucking van I'll . . . I can't believe you were lecturing me before."

He pushed my shoulder. "I said back off, Dub."

I stepped forward. "Don't you fucking push me, Dan," I said, trying to keep my voice level because I knew I was shouting. "Don't you fucking get mad at me because you are dangerously close to fucking this up!"

"Dub," he said slowly, in a dangerous way I recognized as not good, "back off."

I was terrified. My heart was pounding. If Dan swung on me, I would lose a few hours. I stepped back. "I'm driving."

His jaw clenched again. "Fuck you, Dub, I—"

I put a finger against his chest. "No," I said slowly, "fuck *you*. I'm driving. We are not going to blow this because you can't handle a few ugly truths. So fuck you, fuck your god-damned paranoid uncle, and give me the keys."

He was giving me the dead-eyed stare that stupid drunks give you in bars when you're pissing them off, and I was ready to take a blow for the cause. For people like me, being morally right is often all we have.

Dan looked down at his shoes, then at Trim. "Hey, Damien, what do you think?"

I was shocked. I turned to Trim, and he was standing there with his mouth open. He closed it with a click. "I'm sorry, but did you just ask my opinion? Dan, you haven't asked me a real question in months."

Dan was still staring at his feet. "I know. I've been . . . " he swallowed. "I've been an asshole. What do you think?"

Trim threw his hands out dramatically. He didn't say anything for a few moments, but bugged his eyes out, holding his breath. Then all at once he deflated. "Let Dub drive, Dan. He's sobered up. You're red-eyed. You haven't fucked up yet, but you're dangerously close."

Suddenly, we were all making sense.

Dan nodded, and pulled the keys from his pocket. "Saddle up, Dub. It's about a two-hour drive." And he looked at me, and he gave me one of those Saint Dan smiles I hadn't seen in a long time. "But my God, you deserve a kick in the ass."

"Don't worry, I'll handle Uncle Tommy."

We'd been driving in silence for about a half-hour, and we were on Route One in Jersey, just us, the AM radio, and darkness. I had just begun to enjoy the drive, actually, pondering prison and gang homosexual rape and my mother, how she might look through three inches of bulletproof glass.

"Well," I said back, "at least we weren't carrying weapons. They can't charge us with 'armed' robbery, right?"

"True enough," he said quietly.

I liked to drive, although I didn't get much chance to in recent times. Back when I'd had my car, I'd spent most of my time searching for parking spots. Endless nights driving around and around, gazing out at packed streets with pathetic, pale expressions until the morning, when all the other people moved from their spots to go to work. I settled back into the seat and fiddled with the radio. It was all news, sports, and country.

"So, you're going to have ten grand worth of drinks, Danny Boy," I said meanly. "How long does that last?"

He rubbed his eyes tiredly. "Jesus, Dub. We've got two more hours in this van, can't we be nice to each other?"

"Maybe," I conceded, "it would be easier if the radio played something decent. Then I wouldn't have to talk to you."

"We could sing."

I cocked an eyebrow. "I think I'd rather stick pencils in my ears."

"Uh huh. You know, when I was in high school, I had this friend Benny, who owned a little Honda Civic, hatchback."

"You have a rare gift for conversation."

"It had this cloth roof, you know? This padding up on the roof over the metal. It was an old car, and the padding was eaten away, and it used to sag down in our faces. He used a baseball bat to hold the roof up."

"All right, we'll sing. Anything would be—"

Dan was unperturbed. "The point though, was that he had no radio in his car, so we used to sing whenever he drove us places. We'd pick some song that could be done, you know, a capella, and just do the worst fucking job we could think of on it."

"Like what?" I asked.

"That old Cream song, "I Feel Free," used to be one we'd do."

I let that sink in. "I don't want to sing."

"Come on—pick a tune."

"No. I think I've come to appreciate the silence."

"Bullshit."

But we rode in silence for a while anyway, watching the road get darker and more private, eaten away by time. The plan was to drop the truck with Tommy, and when he'd catalogued it and made an estimate, he would give us our cut in cash. We had Dan's assurance that the old con wouldn't cheat us. "He's family," Dan had said simply. "We don't fuck each other. My father'd kill him."

"Sorry if I was hard on you," I finally said.

"Just being honest, right?"

I nodded. "Well, sure. Truth be known, Dan, we've been a little worried about you."

"Nice to hear." He slid down in his seat and leaned back. "But you shouldn't bother. I'm fine. I'm just not as much fun to be around as I used to be. Must be old age."

I sighed. "You want to cling to that hard-ass routine, chum, be my guest. We're concerned, is all."

"Be more concerned whether the po-leece are waiting for us with Tommy in chains, kiddo."

"Egads, that would suck."

And our conversation ended.

We found the intersection Uncle Tommy had specified, and even found Uncle Tommy, unhappy that I was there but resigned, it seemed, to our general incompetence. He took a quick look at our haul, took possession of the van, and told us he would be in touch. Then we were standing in the parking lot alone, rubbing our hands.

"Hey, Dub."

I had a feeling I knew what Dan was about to say. "Yeah?"

"How are we getting home?"

I laughed a little. "Holy shit," I replied, sitting down on the asphalt. "I haven't a fucking clue."

He shook his head. "I'll call Chick, I guess."

I felt a stab of jealousy. "Great. Hey, Dan?"

He turned back, hands searching for change. "Yeah?"

"Where are we?"

His rough laughter rang out, and I just sat and stared at the stoplight, green to yellow to red.

13. The End

I RAN AS HARD AS I'VE EVER RUN, and within three city blocks I was feeling every cigarette and cocktail I'd ever had. But I pushed myself and kept going. I dashed down the streets with an agility and grace I wasn't prepared to discover within myself; it was as if some twelve-year-old version of myself had risen up from the ashtray—and it wasn't until I'd turned onto my street that my heart skipped a beat and I lurched to a sputtering halt, and I wondered what I'd been running from.

I made the rest of the way to my apartment building in a shuffling gasp, filled with phlegm and feeling dead.

Chick Parker was sitting on my front steps, looking perky and well-rested. I stopped and eyed her in silence, taking huge gasps of air. She grinned at me in an insolent way I didn't care for.

"Take your time," she said quietly.

I allowed myself three more herculean breaths. "What are you doing here?"

She blinked at me. "Aren't you happy to find an attractive girl on your steps?"

I bowed my head and felt blood rush into it. "Have you seen Trim or," I gasped, "Dan?"

She nodded. "Yes," she said. "I have."

I waited long enough to feel my lungs come back to what seemed like full size. "And?"

She grinned and stood up. "They're at Rue's. Dan asked me to set a lookout for you, and to bring you."

I let her take my hand, but resisted being moved. "What? Why? We were supposed to meet at Joe Odd's."

"And not invite me? Bad Dub."

"Evil Dub," I agreed. "But it was a boys-only thing, you know?"

"Chest-pounding? Dick-wagging?"

"Something like that."

We walked to Rue's Morgue. In the light, Rue's was free of vampires and almost sunny. It was hard to imagine that Trim and I had spent far too many evenings in there eating darkness and spitting out sarcasm, soaking up fake wisdom and bad meter, not to mention foreign beer. Trim liked to say that domestic beer destroyed ambition, and claimed he only drank domestic beer when it was free.

"They're buying everyone drinks," Chick offered.

"Those idiots," I growled. I felt Chick's eyes on me, and I slid my eyes in her direction. "What?"

"Is this finally over?"

"Is what over?"

"Whatever it is. Whatever's been making you three act premenstrual these past few weeks, months, whatever."

I shrugged. "I think so, Chick."

I waited a moment and then frowned. "Hey?"

"What?"

"Why were you waiting for me? Just because Dan asked you to?" This seemed unlikely; Chick was not a girl who took orders lightly.

She sighed. "All right, take a seat, Dub. I wanted to talk

to you, actually." She indicated the curb outside the bar. I sat down cheerfully, and she perched beside me, elegant in black jeans and army surplus field jacket.

"We're not breaking up, are we?" I asked in my best imitation of good humor. "I knew the sex meant nothing to you."

She gave me a little laugh, and studied the gutter. "Hmmph. Sex is what I need to talk to you about, actually."

My heart started to pound again, and I knew in my heart that I was a coward. I could see the way it ought to be: I was supposed to smile and say I know, and tell her that I was sorry she felt like I needed to be handled gently on this, and give her a kiss, and manage a little dignity. I could see the way it would be, because I found it impossible to say anything, and I could almost feel her trying to will the words out of me. It didn't work.

"Uh huh?" I managed, to let her know I hadn't gone mute.

I could feel her squirming around nervously, and I thought *holy shit, I'm making Chick Parker nervous*. This girl who had made me feel like an idiot for months doesn't know what to say to me. It gave me hope.

"I'm nervous," she said.

"I know," I said, not helping.

"I'm afraid that this is going to open a can of worms."

"Then," I said weakly, "don't bring it up." I couldn't quite connect my morning spent with Norma waiting to get rich with this painful half-conversation that was so depressingly like my life, my life that was supposed to have changed not too long ago.

She looked at me, and I dragged my eyes to hers. It seemed to take hours. "I have to, Dub." She took a deep breath and I looked away just in time.

"Dub, Dan and I—"

"I know."

"You *know*?" she hissed, grabbing my arm and digging her nails in. "Goddamn, that idiot! When did he tell you?"

I opened my mouth.

"And you didn't tell me? You didn't mention it? It didn't bother you? Dub?"

"Do I have a right to be bothered?" The minute I said that, the words haunted me, and I hated myself.

It seemed to slow her down, though. "Uh," she said, and seemed to like the sound of it, since she said it again. "Uh, no, I guess not, Dub." She snorted. "This isn't how this conversation was supposed to go."

"Sorry," I said insincerely. "Chick, if I'm not supposed to be concerned about this, why are you so annoyed that I'm not?"

"I just thought you would be."

"Well," I admitted slowly, "I was. But what's the point?" I studied her feet, big black combat boots that managed to look dainty. "I get real tired of myself sometimes, Chick. I guess I just decided to get over myself, you know?" I looked back at her face. "You seem disappointed that I'd be so mature."

She opened her mouth, then shut it with a click and looked away. "Okay. Fair enough. Sorry, Dub. I got all worked up for this, you know? Didn't you ever expect something to happen, and you summon all your strength to face it, and then it doesn't happen and you're all pumped up with nowhere to go?"

"Like leaning into the wind," I said, "and it stops, and you fall over."

"Yeah!" she said. "I guess I made a fool of myself, huh?"

"Yep," I said happily, and stood up. I offered her my hand. "But that's nothing new. And I've got some business with the boys now, so we'll have to continue this soap opera some other time."

"The boys," she said grimly. "I'm going to kick Dan right in the ass."

"What the hell," I replied. "So am I."

They were sitting at the bar like partisans, toasting each other's good taste in beer and generally acting like insufferable boors, if the look on the bartender's face was to be believed. My eyes found a thick manilla envelope on the bar that Dan was patting in a possessive way. I couldn't believe that the stupid motherfucker had brought it with him, but I decided against violence in a public place, mostly because I knew Dan could kick my ass.

Trim waved us in. "We burst in an hour or two ago shouting that we'd buy the whole place drinks, but there were only three people here, so it lacked drama."

I put my arms around them and stuck my head between theirs. "Maybe," I said menacingly, "if you'd come to Joe Odd's like we'd planned, you would have found a bigger audience, assholes."

Trim blinked at me, then looked over at Chick, who sat next to Dan, then back to me. "Joe Odd's? You must be drunk."

Dan paused with his beer halfway to his lips. "Oops."

I pushed Trim back so I could turn my menace on Dan. "You're despicable."

He looked hurt. "Hey, I said *oops*."

We all laughed, even Chick. "So," she said, giving Dan the cold shoulder, which he didn't even notice, "when do I find out what the hell's been going on with you louts?"

We exchanged looks. Dan shrugged. I shrugged. Trim put an arm around both Dan and Chick and took on an erudite air. "Matters of the world, sweetheart, quite beyond your provincial outlook. The men will have to retire for brandy and cigars to discuss the portents that are beyond your dainty little head."

She looked from me to Trim to Dan, and back to me. "You're not going to tell me, are you?"

"No!" we replied simultaneously. It was one of those weird moments of psychic ability friends can have when they've spent way too much time religiously sharing space, thought, and opinion. It frightened me.

"Fine," she said, sliding off her stool. "You know, I spend too much time in this fucking bar, and too much time trying to figure you morons out. I'm going out to make some new friends."

"You can do that?" Dan asked. "I didn't realize it was an option."

"Fuck you, Dan."

There was a moment of chilly silence as she bustled out the door, and I practiced looking innocent.

"Well," I said eventually, "let me buy you guys a beer. I'm rich, after all."

"Hmmph," Trim snorted. "New money."

My take, all counted, totaled $9,860.00.

That was two years of rent, prepaid. That was four hundred tanks of gas, five thousand trips on the bus to work, six hundred CDs, three thousand cocktails at Rue's (this made me pause in shock), or enough groceries to keep me in Wheaties for years.

If I thought of it as a salary. I'd gotten paid almost ten grand for four months of work, which wasn't bad, but it was only thirty grand a year, really. I didn't know what to make of that.

I set up a schedule of deposits, slipping three hundred dollars in with every paycheck, because I was nervous about all that money being noticed. The rest of the cash I kept, believe it or not, in my toilet, wrapped in plastic and duct tape.

Every time I took a crap, I thought about money.

That night, after we'd sat in Rue's all afternoon laughing and savoring the moment, we did buy everyone drinks. Even Chick, when she came in for her shift. I'd been sitting in one bar or another for twelve hours at that point, and at eleven o'clock, with a light film of Norma still clinging to me, a newly minted rich man, it occurred to me that nothing, really, had changed. Or likely ever would.

I was sitting with people I hadn't seen in a long while, people who, I suspected, had never even dreamed of committing a crime, and I found myself enjoying every vapid moment of the conversation. Free of deep thoughts and endless planning, not to mention the endless responsibility of everyone's precious heart. I looked around, and there was Dan, sitting at the bar, talking to Chick while she blatantly goofed off while on the job. On the other side of the room, enthralling some newly minted cronies with his ancient and blackened oratory, was Trim. He noticed me watching him and gave me a wink, and went back to enraging his listeners with some extraordinary line of bullshit or other.

And I realized that we were never going to be close again.

Drifting or not, we ended up back at my place at six in the morning to have a nightcap, and then to crash. I had a bottle of old scotch my mom had given me years before, and I poured the three of us a finger or two, and we stood in my living room, drank it down, and went to sleep.

14. Epilogue

I ran into Trim at McCellan's Pub on Amsterdam. We'd both been out for quite some time, apparently, and literally bumped into each other on the way to the bathroom. We both exclaimed that we looked like shit. Out of the men's room, we sat down at the bar away from our other friends and bought each other gimlets. Trim was dressed in his traditional black, with the boisterous exception of the most ridiculously floral tie I'd ever seen.

"How've you been, Dub?" he asked.

"The same, I guess," I said. "I guess I haven't been around much, huh?"

"Wouldn't know," he said, and laughed. "Are you rich yet?"

"No. You?"

"In the complicated process of pissing it all away, friend," he said with a serious wink. "It isn't easy, you know. I make it look easy. But it isn't easy."

"What's with the tie?" I asked, wisely deciding to ignore this obvious baiting.

"I'm going straight. It's a process, you know. You've got to take it slowly, step by step."

"Bullshit."

He raised a tired blonde eyebrow at me. "No, what's

bullshit is hanging out in the same fucking bar every goddamn night."

"And going straight means hanging out in a completely
different bar?"

He hit me lightly on the head, which I took well. "No,
my little idiot bastard. This is special. I'm celebrating."

"What?"

"Nothing," he said with a few sighs that cracked me up,
"in particular."

We sat for a moment. "How's Dan?"

He shrugged. "No one's seen him. You still working?"

I nodded with a sheepish smile. "At the same place."

He shook his head. "Dub, Dub, Dub . . . I am very disappointed."

So was I. But not-exactly-ten-grand didn't make me in-
dependently wealthy. We sat again, for a few moments this
time, until my cigarette had burned down and my gimlet
was just ice. "Well," I said, standing up, "I should get back."

"Yeah," he agreed. "Dub? Stay cool."

I smiled and looked at my shoes. "Never was, brother."

I turned and heard Trim snort behind me. "And never
will be!"

And I don't think we ever saw each other again.

JEFF SOMERS WAS BORN AND RAISED IN JERSEY CITY, NEW JERSEY, WHERE HE CURRENTLY STILL LIVES. HE BEGAN WRITING AFTER AN INCIDENT OF SEVERE HEAD TRAUMA WHEN HE WAS TEN YEARS OLD, AND LATER GRADUATED FROM RUTGERS UNIVERSITY UNDER MYSTERIOUS CIRCUMSTANCES, WITH NO MEMORY OF THE INTERVENING TWELVE YEARS. AFTER GRADUATION, HE DROVE CROSS COUNTRY IN HIS BLUE CHEVY NOVA AND EXPERIENCED A LIFE CHANGING EPIPHANY AND HAS NOT LEFT THE HOUSE SINCE, SPENDING HIS TIME IN HIS BATHROBE AND PAJAMAS, SMOKING CIGARETTES AND DRINKING HIGHBALLS. THE NEIGHBORHOOD KIDS REFER TO HIM AS "BATHROBE MAN" AND THROW ROCKS AT HIM WHENEVER HE APPEARS ON HIS PORCH TO COLLECT NEWSPAPERS OR LIQUOR DELIVERIES. IN 1995 HE BEGAN PUBLISHING HIS OWN ZINE, THE INNER SWINE, WHICH HAS BEEN MET WITH RESOUNDING DISINTEREST AND INTERNATIONAL OBSCURITY. THE PICTURE SHOWN HERE IS THE MOST RIDICULOUS PHOTO HE COULD FIND, AND THUS PLEASES HIM GREATLY. HE IS UNIVERSALLY CONSIDERED TO LOOK GOOD IN TIGHT PANTS, AND HE SOMETIMES HUMS TO HIMSELF IN PUBLIC.